The Golden Oldies' Club

MARK DAYDY

ISBN: 9798837655395

Cover design by MIKE DAYDY

CONTENTS

1

Sign Here

Jo Ramsey couldn't take her eyes off 'Friday' on the calendar – specifically, the final entry in the box below it.

Big changes were coming.

What she needed was a distraction. She'd feel better if she thought about something else.

Work! That was the best distraction of all. It was always busy at marketing firm A. J. Bonner, and Wednesday mornings in early June were no exception. She couldn't waste time fretting about Friday. Not with schedules to fix, meetings to arrange…

Laughter interrupted her thoughts. Middle-aged fellow admin staff Annette and Amy were sharing something hilarious.

Jo envied them. They were never short of a distraction. Then again, they didn't have to worry about…

Her gaze returned to the calendar and Friday's final entry.

'4 p.m. Retirement Party.'

Unhelpfully, a retirement-related disaster from three years ago broke the surface like the shark in Jaws.

She did her best to ignore it by focusing on the many positives. After a lifetime of employment, she would be free to pursue a wide range of fascinating activities such as... that's to say, fun things along the lines of... or to be absolutely specific, worthwhile interests in the nature of...

Pottery.

She had no idea why she'd thought that.

Desperation, probably.

Dismissing it, she poured bottled water into the soil of the large aspidistra by her desk and eyed the tray of chocolate cupcakes on the low cabinet beside it. Handing out birthday treats was an obligation she had met every year since joining Bonner's at Avalon House in her twenties.

So...

Rising from her seat, she smoothed down her beige blouse and midnight blue skirt. Her silver hair, although short and neat, also got a flattening. With the morning coffee break almost upon them, it was time.

"Birthday cupcake, anyone?" she asked, lifting the tray.

While most raised a hand and waved, dyed blonde Annette and copper-haired Amy arrived like human lightning bolts, instantaneously swiping a cake apiece and taking a bite while dispensing birthday wishes.

"Only two days to freedom," said Annette, offering an excellent view of her half-full mouth.

"Can you imagine never having to get up for work?" said Amy, wiping her lips with her fingers.

"Ooh, getting up late..."

"A lazy breakfast..."

"Shopping while everyone else is at work..."

"A relaxing lunch..."

"A nap?" They laughed before Annette continued. "Afternoon TV, a good book, out to dinner…"

"And an early or late night to be decided as you please, Jo."

She smiled along with them – outwardly.

Inwardly, she felt a strong desire to shove cupcakes in their faces.

"I can hardly wait," she said before handing out cakes to those polite enough to remain at their desks.

A few moments later, she headed off to the other half of the fourth-floor team who inhabited another office.

Floor-to-ceiling windows flanked one side of the corridor between the two offices. For those not in a hurry, it offered a tantalising view of the sea a mile and a half away.

Here, Jo paused.

Forty years…

Under a cobalt sky, sunlight glinted off distant calm waters. A few yachts dotted the seascape while a small white plane trailed an advertisement somewhere near the beach. Situated on southern England's famed Jurassic Coast, Tolcombe was undeniably a beautiful place, but to no longer have this view of it…?

Forget it! While everyone else is stuck in the office, a certain lucky person will be lazing around, feet up, drink in hand, living the dream, for the rest of her days.

Entering the other office, she beheld forty-something 3D artist Scott swivelling in his chair while on the phone. Bessie used to sit there. She never swivelled.

Jo checked herself. She wasn't the grumpy type. No need to start being one this close to the finish line.

"Birthday cupcake, anyone?"

Several hands shot up.

"Happy sixty-sixth," said Kim, a gruff fifty-something admin co-worker who emitted a strong waft of mint and tobacco whenever she spoke. "How are you feeling?"

Like I'm on the Titanic and I've just spotted an iceberg.

"Oh, I'm fine, thanks," said Jo as Kim took a cake.

She next headed for Milly the temp, who was fresh out of college but looked no older than twelve. Forty years in admin had meant navigating the arrival of email, PowerPoint, and Zoom. What kind of future awaited these young ones?

"Thanks," said Milly, taking a cake.

"Going well?" Jo asked.

Milly smiled self-consciously.

"Just filling in job applications. If I can get a bunch of interviews, I'll hopefully have my pick."

"That sounds like a plan," said Jo, although not a plan she would have ever enacted herself.

"I shouldn't, I shouldn't," said beanpole graphic designer Nina, coming over to take a cake.

"I know, I know," said Jo watching her get started by nibbling off the topping.

Nina's recent birthday had been marked with a huge chocolate gateau topped with a '30' motif.

"Don't tell me how many calories," she said with a conspiratorial wink.

It's 340, but okay.

The last of the cakes went to Jennifer, a sophisticated sixty-one-year-old colleague who would be retiring a few months after Jo.

"Mmm, lovely. Thank you and Happy Birthday."

"Thanks, Jen."

Jo liked Jennifer. She was always immaculately dressed, while her long auburn hair was never anything less than radiant. Nothing had been confirmed but she was hoping

4

they might become retirement buddies who enjoyed a monthly coffee together.

Making her way back along the corridor, Jo paused to take in the view once more. Any inner calm she might have gained though was disrupted by young Ollie from HR coming through the stairwell doors.

"Ah, our retiree-to-be," he said. "We just need your autograph on a couple of documents."

Obviously, she could have bashed him with the empty cake tray and fled – but she simply placed it against the wall to pick up later.

Following him down the concrete stairwell to the third floor, she knew she didn't have to retire at all. The law protected her.

Yay!

Except, not yay.

In a month or so, Bonner's would be relocating to new offices on the other side of Bournemouth – a.k.a. a commute that would turn her into an extra from Zombies Unleashed.

Not that she had to physically travel every day if she didn't want to. She could work from home two days a week.

Yay again!

Except, not yay again.

She had no desire to work from home. Any pleasure she derived from performing admin tasks was inextricably linked to spending time with living, breathing colleagues, and not from seeing their little faces on a laptop screen in her kitchen-diner.

"Right," said Ollie as they reached the HR office.

"Hello Jo, how are you feeling?" Ollie's colleague, Trish asked.

I wish people would stop asking how I'm feeling.

"I'm fine, Trish. Thanks for asking."

She wished she had felt fine, just like the millions who saw retirement as freedom rather than an ending – but, come Monday, she would be living it for the rest of her life, so would simply have to adapt.

Just then, the disaster from three years back surfaced again. Only, this time she couldn't force it down.

Retirement? For the rest of her life?

Three years ago, she lost her husband, Martin, when he suffered a heart attack four weeks into *his* retirement.

"If you could just check them over," said Ollie, indicating two printed documents.

"It all looks fine," said Jo with barely a glance.

"Are you sure you don't want me to arrange a consultation?" Ollie added. "The company's happy to pay."

"No, I'm fine, thank you."

She wanted to take the next few weeks at her own pace, and not have anyone pushing her to do things she wouldn't be interested in.

"Okay," said Ollie, "so if you could just sign there… and there."

Suddenly, all the feelings of trepidation rushed to grip her innards and constrict her chest. She felt hot and sweaty. Her heart thumped.

There were doubts.

No, that was nonsense. She was simply moving on. It happened every day all over the world. She was retiring from work. It was no big deal.

"Everything alright?" asked Ollie.

Hot and sweaty turned to cold and clammy.

"Yes… yes… everything's absolutely fine."

Her pen hovered.

It was just a couple of signatures. She could manage that, couldn't she?

2

Park Life

At lunchtime, Jo shut her computer down and locked a few paper documents in the drawer. It was a company requirement as some of the materials she worked with were confidential. That said, it was hard to imagine who might see her screen or papers through a fourth-floor window.

"Just popping out," she informed the office – which was currently made up of Amy talking on the phone and Annette munching on a triple-decker sandwich while checking entertainment news on her desktop screen.

Jo took the stairs down, as she often did. She was going to miss all this, but it wasn't just the end of *her* tenure at Avalon House. For some time, there had been a mood at board level of the old place no longer fitting the company's brand.

In contrast, Skyline was a group of twelve fresh, modern, glass and steel units. Bonner's new home would be at Number 10, and they would have it all to themselves. For sure, things would never be the same.

Outside, it was a beautiful summer's day with just a hint of a breeze. Funny how such fabulous weather was almost inconsequential in the office. She sucked in a lungful of fresh air before setting off.

Beyond the car park, she spotted the tanned shaved head of her boss, Terry. He was with a couple of colleagues – no doubt heading off for a swift pub lunch. Despite only being in his late-thirties, Terry had an incredibly mature outlook – and he'd been brilliant lately, making a fuss and keeping her nicely busy. It had been a pleasure to work for him over the past four years. How many bosses had she had at Bonner's? Eleven? Twelve?

A few minutes later, reaching a busy Park Street, aromas of fresh bread from the Crusty Cob artisan bakers and fresh coffee from the fashionable Bubble & Squeak café assailed her nostrils. Not that she stopped. She had a flask of tea, a few grapes, and a cheddar cheese sandwich wrapped in tinfoil.

She pushed on, past the yellow and white striped awning of the florist, past the delivery men wrestling a new refrigerator into the deli, and past the burger bar, where two of Bonner's young third floor workers waved to her from their window seats.

She waved back. For young people, Bonner's was a good company, with its range of clients – charities, non-governmental organizations, corporations – and its variety of output, from making short safety films and explainer videos to producing promotional brochures and internet campaigns. There was a lot more to it than just admin.

Tolcombe Park greeted her with a rainbow of floral hues across the various shaped beds, while a variety of mature trees quivered with the songs of sparrows, finches, and robins.

A spaniel ran past; its owner calling after it. Indeed, thanks to the sunshine, a fair number of people were enjoying a lunchtime escape. Some were sunbathing, others strolled, while a few jogged – although surely it was too hot for that.

Jo took it all in. It truly was glorious.

Taking to a bench by the pond, she unwrapped her sandwich.

Ah, this is the life…

She took a bite and began to chew thoughtfully while watching the ducks. The peace it brought was almost zen-like.

It didn't last though.

Big Ben…?

It wasn't *the* Big Ben, obviously, which stood more than a hundred miles away in London, but someone on the other side of the water dressed as the world-famous clock tower. He or she… or it… was helping a dragon to push a shopping trolley.

Jo unscrewed her flask and poured a little tea into the plastic cup. No doubt it was students messing around to get likes on YouTube.

"Hello Jo."

A slim, silver-haired woman in her late sixties was coming down the path.

"Hello Marilyn. How are you?"

"I'm good, thanks. How about you?"

"Yes, fine, fine."

Living just a street apart, their occasional bumping into each other over the past twenty years or so had evolved into a kind of friendship.

"How's work?" Marilyn asked, taking a space on the bench.

"Funny you should ask…" It wasn't lost on Jo that her friend had retired from her office role at the county court a couple of years ago and seemed to be doing well. "Things have happened."

"Oh?"

"Have you ever had your hand start shaking when you're expected to sign something?"

"What's happened, Jo?" Marilyn's voice was full of concern.

"I'm retiring."

"Really?" Marilyn seemed genuinely surprised.

"Yes, on Friday."

"Well… that's great. Hopefully, it'll work out this time."

"Yes, I'm sure it will. I expect I'll be swamped by all the things I'll be free to do."

Feeling a little awkward, she pondered pottery as a logical first hobby to try. It would help her to be creative while maintaining dexterity in later years. Although wasn't wet clay bad for rheumatism and arthritis…?

"Are you sure you're alright, Jo?"

"Yes, yes, I'm fine. I could have stayed on, but the company's relocating to the other side of Bournemouth."

"Oh, not a commute for the faint-hearted."

"No, instead of a fifteen-minute walk to work, it's two buses in non-moving traffic plus twenty minutes walking."

"I don't suppose the train would have solved anything?"

"Not with the stations being nowhere near home or the new office."

"Right."

"And as for taking a cab – we're talking appalling traffic and fares that would wipe out half my net income."

Marilyn shrugged in an 'oh well' kind of way.

"We're the same age, aren't we," she said. "I had my sixty-eighth last month."

"Mine's today."

"Oh, happy birthday."

"Thank you."

Yes, Jo Ramsey was sixty-eight and proud of it, although she was happy for colleagues at Bonner's to think she was a little younger.

"Obviously, it's not easy to leave work behind," she said. "I've enjoyed being in a busy office." *Year after year. Decade after decade.* "But I'm looking forward to a new phase now. Very much so."

Nonetheless, Marilyn must have picked up on some aspect of uncertainty.

"Retirement can be a funny old thing. Not everyone packs up work on a Friday and, by Monday, is arranging dozens of activities with lots of friends. For most people, it's something to ease ourselves into."

"That's exactly what I plan to do."

Jo sipped her tea and tried to focus on the ducks. Like her they were serene on top, busy below the surface.

"Have you thought of attending a retirement seminar?" Marilyn suggested. "Or there are some really good books on the subject."

"I'll be fine. I've already had a few ideas and I've even got a date lined up for tonight."

"Oh well, that's lovely."

"He's a friend of Martin's."

"That's nice. Someone you can trust."

"Yes."

"It's good to see you're on top of the situation. It's just, for some, we can lose our sense of purpose… which can undermine confidence."

Jo nodded. "As I say, I'm fine."

"I'm glad. It took me a while, but luckily I fell in with a lovely bunch of fellow retirees."

"Oh right – that's good."

"It is. If you're ever at a loose end, you could join us for a coffee morning. The initiation ceremony's quite simple. It's blood rites."

"Pardon me?"

"Just kidding. It's usually lattes and cake. Why don't I introduce you to a few of them? They're only over there."

Jo's eyes widened. Marilyn seemed to be indicating Big Ben and the dragon. Only now, these two loons were being chased by a large woman dressed as a pirate.

Worse still, Marilyn was calling them over.

And even more alarmingly, they were waving back and making their way around from the other side of the pond.

"Hiya!" hollered Big Ben, his face sticking out through a clockface hole in the cardboard. This was no student prankster.

"Rrrr," the dragon roared. And neither was this.

"Don't worry," said Marilyn, "the trolley's borrowed, not stolen. It's meant to be the Houses of Parliament, but things weren't ready in time."

But Jo didn't want to meet clock towers, dragons, or pirates during her lunch break. She wanted to sort out her retirement in her own way and in her own time.

Balancing speed with a desire to not offend, she packed her half-eaten lunch into her bag and prepared to dispose of her paper tissue… only her move for the bin took the human clock tower by surprise and they collided.

"I'm so sorry," said Big Ben.

"Meet Owen," said Marilyn.

"I think his costume's a bit unwieldy," said the dragon. "I'm Ruth, by the way, and our pirate is Yvonne."

"Yo-ho-ho," puffed the slightly breathless buccaneer arriving with a friendly wave of her cardboard cutlass.

"Are you sure you're alright?" Owen enquired, "I'm such an oaf."

"I'm sure it was just bad timing," said Yvonne. "Do you get it? He's a clock."

Jo was unable to think of a sensible reply although she toyed with insisting he keep his 'hands' to himself.

"Everyone, this is my friend Jo," said Marilyn. "Jo, meet the Go Club."

"It's short for the Golden Oldies' Club," Ruth explained.

"It's not an official club," said Owen. "It's just what we call ourselves."

Jo thought a better name might be the Meddling Nutters' Club.

"It was nearly called the Bubble & Squeak Club," said Yvonne, "after a chic little café where the originals held their first get-together."

"But we couldn't," said Ruth. "Without the fashionable irony, Bubble & Squeak is a dish of reheated leftovers."

"I think it describes us perfectly," said Yvonne.

"Jo's retiring on Friday," Marilyn said, changing the subject, "and today's her birthday."

Jo knew she would implode should they launch into the birthday song, but mercifully they kept it to some hearty salutations.

Meanwhile, Big Ben removed the top section of his outfit from his shoulders.

"Are you sure you're alright?" he asked.

Under ruffled silver hair, his eyes were kindly and engaging. Jo couldn't recall the last time a man looked at her in such a warm and open way.

"Yes, fine…" she said before something occurred to her.

She knew him from somewhere.

"I really am sorry," he apologised once again.

Jo felt something odd – a mild but definite rising emotion in her chest. And she could name it too, although it was too ridiculous for words. Her first experience of it had come more than half a century ago with long-haired, flared-trousered Keith. But this was a man, possibly in his late sixties, wedged into a homemade clock tower. It made even less sense as she had finally given in to Eddie's request that they get together. Eighteen months he'd been asking her to have dinner or go to the cinema – and tonight would be their first date. So, to have Big Ben provoke such a reaction… well, clearly, she was losing her marbles.

"I really ought to be getting back to the office," she said.

Of course, she knew where to place the blame. If retirement were a person, he'd be a sneaky so-and-so, luring her away from her beloved job like the child-catcher in *Chitty Chitty Bang Bang*. She wondered what other trickery retirement had up its sleeve. Clearly, she would have to be on her guard.

3

Thoughts of Martin… and Eddie… and Big Ben

Arriving home at her semi-detached house in South Tolcombe, Jo closed the front door against the world. It had been a long day.

Taking off her shoes in the fawn-carpeted hallway, she glanced in the long mirror. Having gone up soon after she and Martin moved in forty years ago, it had seen her turn slowly from a dark-haired, carefree young woman into a more reserved senior citizen. It had also witnessed their son William growing up, and the paramedics treating Martin on the floor.

That mirror had seen it all.

After work, she usually enjoyed a simple meal and some time in front of the TV. As a fan of cookery shows and detective mysteries, she often watched one of each most evenings. It felt odd to think she'd soon be able to watch them all day long for the rest of her life.

Tonight though, she had a date with Eddie.

She placed her shoes on the chrome rack, which contained her other three pairs, all of which could be categorised as comfortable footwear.

"Well, one pair of you is coming out tonight whether you like it or not."

She grabbed the pair with the highest heels: black loafers that would raise her up an entire inch. A quick polish and they would do.

Going through to the kitchen-diner, she put the kettle on and glanced at this week's list of convenience meals pinned to the fridge by a Marge Simpson magnet. A solo chicken pie, farmhouse pizza, tuna pasta bake, spaghetti Bolognese, cod fishfingers, veggie burgers, and a Cornish pasty. Had the Eddie thing fallen through, she would have had the Bolognese.

Armed with a hot cup of tea, she went upstairs to the second bedroom. Here, with the back of the house facing southwest, strong sunshine flooded through the net curtain. This had been their son's old room.

Memories of William growing up came to her, as they often did. Unidentifiable Lego structures, off-key flute practice, pretending to be a space ranger... and much later, exam revision and strange ambient music...

After William left home for university in Manchester, it became Martin's office. Here, the memories blended into one – that of Martin at his computer corresponding on seemingly vital matters as vice-chair of a local citizens group.

Sometimes, when the room was quiet, she half-expected a three-year-old William to call her or, more likely, Martin to come in muttering about bureaucracy and inefficiency.

Poor Martin. He only got as far as his fourth week of retirement from the insurance industry. A couple of weeks before this, he persuaded her to retire early to be at his side. Sadly, just days after handing in her resignation, Fate intervened.

Following a swift withdrawal of her notice, Avalon House provided such emotional comfort that when her state pension became payable, she held off taking it for two more years. In fact, had Bonner's not been about to move, she might have stayed on until they carried her out in a wooden box.

She placed her tea on the empty chest of drawers and went to the window. In the garden below, nothing stirred, although a blue tit was having a whale of a time splashing in next door's bird bath.

Oh, to be as carefree as you.

She checked her watch.

Plenty of time.

She and Eddie would have dinner at a restaurant and then…

And then?

Would they go back to his place? No, that would be like one of those horror movies where a teen enters a haunted house.

No, she and Eddie would enjoy a pleasant meal and then… well, she would deal with 'and then' should it arise. Although, with her being sixty-eight and Eddie seventy-three, perhaps the physical side of things would be limited to a goodnight handshake.

The doorbell rang.

"Eddie…?"

She hurried downstairs to open the door to…

"Marilyn…?"

This was most odd – despite living close by, she had never called at Jo's house before.

"Sorry to bother you… and sorry about lunchtime. They're a good bunch though, aren't they?"

"Yes, um, would you like to come in? I could rustle up some tea or coffee?"

"Only if it's not too much trouble."

Plenty of time, plenty of time…

"The kettle's just boiled. Let me get my tea from upstairs and I'll meet you in the kitchen. It's just through there."

Five minutes later they were seated at the pine table in her kitchen-diner sipping hot drinks.

"So, the Go Club," said Jo.

"Yes, I think Ruth mentioned it's short for the Golden Oldies' Club."

"Yes – so what were they up to in the park?"

"It's the carnival soon and we're doing a charity walk as part of it. They were just trying out their costumes for size."

"Are you part of it?"

"Yes, I was meant to be a tiger, but the delivery's been delayed."

"Ah, so they're all new costumes then?"

"Not all of them, but it's been a year since the last fancy dress walk, and some of us tend to change size over time."

"Yes, well… I liked the Big Ben costume."

She thought it best to leave out having a schoolgirl reaction to the man inside it. At sixty-eight, a woman needed to hang on to her standards.

"Yes, Owen… Owen Tate. He's a retired actor. Stage and television."

"Oh really?" So that's where she had seen him before – on TV. "How exciting."

"He had lots of small roles but was never the star."

"I knew I'd seen him somewhere."

"Yes, he was in some big shows. He did EastEnders a couple of times."

"He's certainly a celebrity then. I can imagine he has some stories to tell."

"Ah, if it's scandal you're after, you're out of luck. He never says a bad word about anyone."

"I'm glad to hear it. He did seem nice."

"Ah-ha, I know what you're after."

A shot of embarrassment coursed through Jo's veins. Was it that obvious?

Marilyn smiled.

"I'm sure he'd sign a photo."

"Ah… yes, a signed photo. Does he do a lot of that kind of thing?"

"Not so much these days, although he once had a middle-aged woman ask him to sign her boob."

"Oh," said Jo, trying to avoid picturing it. "I suppose the loyalty of a fan deserves reward."

"On the subject of men, didn't you mention having a date lined up?"

"Yes. Eddie. It's our first date tonight."

"Oh right. Well, I won't stay long then…"

Jo sipped her tea. Eddie was fine. And honestly – people going around autographing other people's body parts… it just wasn't the done thing. Clearly, when it came to fanciful thoughts, she would have to call time on Big Ben.

*

The doorbell chimed at a quarter to seven. Eddie was fifteen minutes early. Jo wasn't too keen on that. This wasn't a business meeting where being early was advisable. This was a date. He knew she'd be getting ready. What was he hoping for? A flash of her undergarments? No, that was silly. He was a respected elder in the community.

"You don't mind me being early, do you?" he asked in a sing-song voice that swamped any opportunity for dissent.

"No, absolutely not," said Jo, recoiling at the strength of his after-shave and wondering if he bathed in it.

She had to admit though – he looked good in a tan blazer and open-necked white shirt. He'd also had his silver hair cropped super short, which suited him.

"I must say, you look smart, Eddie."

"That's exactly what my neighbour said."

"Compliments from neighbours. That's nice."

"She's eighty-odd and lives alone. Nothing better to do than spy on people."

"Yes, well, I'm almost ready. Why don't you take a seat in the living room?"

Showing him in, she wondered if she might become a nosy old neighbour with nothing better to do than spy on people.

"It's only a ten-minute walk," he said, "but probably best to wear good shoes. I'm getting a bit too old to carry anyone."

"Where are we going?"

"Giovanni's. It's in the middle of Upper Street."

Upper Street was less than half a mile southeast of Jo's place, by the High Point cliffs and the beach.

"Lovely," she said.

Slipping on her chosen shoes, she tried to get into the right frame of mind for her first date since losing Martin. Eddie was eight years into retirement from a management role at a kitchen installation firm. He had practical, first-hand knowledge of how to survive. In many ways, he was a sensible choice.

Of course, there was still that little anxiety inside her, that she might be getting this all wrong.

4

Date Night

Entering Giovanni's, Jo surmised that Wednesday evenings weren't the Italian restaurant's busiest. Despite the neat little bar, the array of unusual spirits, the racks of wine, and the jars of decorative oils on display, only two other couples had been lured inside. It was a lovely, warm atmosphere though, with gentle piano music in the background and the sounds and smells of interesting cooking coming from somewhere out of sight at the back. Just the thing for a relaxing dinner date.

"Our usual table in the nook," said Eddie, pointing to it for the benefit of the waiter.

The waiter swiftly overcame any puzzlement and showed them to the table between the wall and a pillar. Not technically a nook, but clearly the most private seating on offer.

"We don't want the paparazzi spotting us," Eddie added.

Jo smiled as they were handed a menu each. This was obviously his way of making her feel at ease.

"We're looking for a regular haunt," he informed the waiter. "I assume the service is top notch?"

"Of course, sir. Would you like to order drinks before dinner?"

"Mine's a bottled lager. Jo?"

"Oh, um…" Up until that moment, she hadn't given any thought to alcohol and its power to lay waste to people's inhibitions. "A small gin and tonic, please, and a large glass of water."

"Ice and lemon with both?"

"Yes, please. Lots of ice."

"You wanna try lime with the gin," said Eddie.

"Yes, alright."

The waiter smiled at Jo and turned to Eddie. "And water for you too, sir?"

"Never touch the stuff."

Jo grinned with mild embarrassment. No doubt, a large tip would be in order come the end of the evening.

"Soon be the tourist season," said Eddie watching the waiter retreat. "We want to make sure we get priority when it's busy."

She admired his belief that this would be a regular thing.

"Let's hope it's a good summer," she said.

"Jo, you deserve the best time. You deserve to feel special, to feel appreciated. You deserve the best retirement, the best life. It's what Martin would have wanted. And if in some tiny way I can help you with that, then I'm here for you."

"That's… nice. Thank you."

She first met twice-divorced Eddie at a golf awards dinner twenty years ago. He used to play with Martin and others at a local course and, occasionally, in Portugal.

He first asked her out on a date eighteen months ago and had done so again on two further occasions. She had declined each time, but when he suggested it a couple of weeks ago, she wondered if he might be what she needed in retirement. It was a thought based largely on hope rather than expectation. In truth, she wondered if she was trying to fix her retirement anxiety by installing a partner. That said, what else could she do but give him a chance? After all, he and Martin had been close friends.

The waiter returned with their drinks, which he set out before them.

"Thank you," said Jo.

He seemed to appreciate it, smiling back at her.

"I'll have the garlic mushrooms and Bolognese," said Eddie without looking at the menu.

"And signora?" the waiter enquired.

"Oh… um…"

"I can come back?" he offered.

"No, it's alright. I'll have the same, thank you."

Note to self – move the microwaveable Bolognese from fridge to freezer.

Having noted their orders on a pad, the waiter thanked them and took the menus away with him.

"Cheers," said Eddie, reaching over to clink his beer bottle against her gin and tonic.

"Cheers," she replied.

She enjoyed the hit of icy botanical gin and lime on her tongue, so at least he was right about not going for the lemon. But more importantly, he held retirement in the palm of his hand, so this was an opportunity to learn something.

"Make sure you're getting your state pension without delay," he said while pouring his beer into the glass.

"It's all in hand," she said. She had delayed taking it at sixty-six and would now get a larger monthly payment. Also, she would be getting her Bonner's pension and their fairly substantial tax-free lump sum.

"What you want is a nice getaway. Somewhere like the Caribbean. By all means get used to your new way of life first but when you're ready, drop everything and go. Just remember to grab a friend to take along with you. It'll be fun."

"Possibly," said Jo, but she wasn't too sure about that.

"Travel is good for the soul," Eddie opined. "Do you ever watch those cookery shows where they go abroad? Italy, France, Greece?"

"Yes, I do."

"Cooking always looks fun on TV."

"Yes, although I'm not sure I'd be any good at making any of the dishes."

She certainly had none of Gordon Ramsey's passion, which probably explained why her meals were always bland. Not that it had bothered Martin. He'd lived his whole life as a basic meat and two veg man. Throughout their marriage, whatever meal she placed before him, he unfailingly added a splodge of brown sauce. He didn't like garlic or chilli. Jo couldn't even have it back in the days when she used to go out with friends as he'd have detected it on her breath and made a fuss.

But Eddie was right, wasn't he? Cooking exotic dishes did look fun on TV.

"What's the first thing that comes to mind when you think about food?" he asked.

The buffet choices for her retirement party came to mind.

"Um…?"

"Love," he said with a smile.

"Love?" Her guard activated like a Star Trek alien-repelling forcefield.

"Love of food," he added.

Jo nodded with relief. The thought of being in love with Eddie did not sit well with her. He was a companion. He would help her ease into a successful retirement. That was enough, wasn't it?

"I love Italian food," he said.

As he launched into an analysis of the menu choices, she tried to see the whole picture. He was a man. Men liked... well, she knew what men liked. But Eddie was different. He was seventy-three. Didn't men pack it in once they reached sixty? Martin, her beloved husband packed it in at fifty-one when she was in her late forties. Although now she thought of it, she hadn't been particularly thrilled at the time.

"You've lived a full life, Jo," said Eddie, jolting her out of her reverie. "Tell me some of things that stand out for you. Cherished memories. Anything you like."

It seemed odd. Did he think getting her to talk about herself would win her over? Perhaps it would.

She thought of telling him about her first days at Bonner's, when she was fresh and young. The people she worked with back then...

As it was, Eddie rose from his chair.

"Just need to spend a penny."

"Ah right."

While he was gone, she changed her mind. She didn't want to talk about work. Perhaps she'd share a story from her childhood. Although, which one?

It came to her...

A tiny cove in Devon. She was with her parents. Her dad was fishing. She wandered off up a path. Her mum shouted to stay away from the edge. This would have been in the mid-1960s when she was around twelve. She followed the path over a crest and down to another tiny cove. And she stood there, on a flat rock, a hundred yards from her parents. For one precious moment, she was the only person on earth. She tried to imagine how the coming days and weeks might go. What would she eat? Where would she sleep? She wasn't scared. It was a daydream that gave her a tremendous sense of joyful curiosity. Over the years, she often wondered about that feeling, because it had proven hard to find again.

Eddie eventually returned and dropped into his seat with a satisfied sigh.

"Right…"

Jo was about to tell him of her childhood memory, but he must have forgotten the thread because he asked if she could drive.

"Oh… well… I have a license. But I haven't driven in years."

"I'm between cars," he explained. "I sold a nice Jaguar a while back and haven't been able to settle on a replacement."

"Oh."

Her last car had really been her husband's. A lovely silver Honda Civic. But she sold it after he died.

"Driving gives you freedom," said Eddie. "You should consider getting a little run-around."

"Possibly."

Even before the first course had arrived, she knew he wasn't her type. But she was sixty-eight and very much drawn to his confidence in dealing with the thing that concerned her most. And, at the back of her mind, she knew Martin would approve of him.

5

The Right Man…?

Jo and Eddie were seated opposite each other in her living room finishing off an end-of-date coffee.

"Very homely, your place," he observed. "I mean that in a positive sense. I feel right at home here."

Jo dipped into the box of thin chocolate mints. Eddie didn't have a sweet tooth, so was leaving her to it.

"I've always tried to make it comfortable," she said, aware that she kept glancing at the clock on the mantelpiece, and that the transition from ten o'clock to five past had seemingly taken half an hour.

"Nice décor," he said.

"Thanks."

She tried and failed to prevent thoughts popping into her head. What would happen if they were sitting on the sofa come eleven? Awkward stuff?

Possibly.

Adult activities?

Not a chance. At least not on a first date.

So, on a second date?

Definitely not.

A twentieth date?

Possibly.

So, realistically, getting it together physically with Eddie would happen between this and their twentieth date. At least that narrowed it down a bit. It also posed an important question. What would be worse? Making love with Eddie or commuting to Bonner's new offices?

He came to sit beside her on the sofa and pecked her on the cheek. It felt like being assessed by a ninja assassin, but surely she had to allow the occasional kiss. It wouldn't be viable to continue as companions without sporadic displays of affection.

"Mmm," he said, although she wasn't sure why. Perhaps he hadn't eaten enough at the restaurant.

"The food at Giovanni's was lovely tonight," she said.

"Mmm."

He kissed her again, only this time he shifted position so that his lips could linger on hers. She supposed it was a moment where she might have sensed a trace of passion in her heart, but she could only detect garlic and coffee on his breath. Was that a win for Martin's logic? Or just the result of Eddie not going for the chocolate mints?

"That's the first restaurant Bolognese I've had in decades," she said.

"Mmm," he replied as he kissed her once more.

"So much nicer than the one I've got in the fridge…" *which I must put in the freezer!*

Out of nowhere, a question came to her. What if he had a heart attack while they were…?

Would his thing deflate? Or would rigor mortis mean…?

Would the fire brigade have to be called?

Note to self. Keep phone within easy reach.

Actually, there was another important question. How would it be after twenty years of abstinence? It was becoming clear that she hadn't thought this through at all.

Eddie's hand was suddenly and unexpectedly on her shoulder. How did it get there? She hadn't noticed it move. It slid off the shoulder and down her arm. It was now on her bare skin.

"Seven o'clock," she blurted.

"Sorry?"

"I have to be up at seven o'clock for work."

She forced out a yawn.

"It's not even ten past ten," he pointed out.

"Yes, but it's been such a hectic day. I really do have to say goodnight."

"Absolutely. Of course. Everything's alright though?"

"How do you mean?"

"Well, we're not dead yet."

"No…" she said, "but I do have a busy day ahead."

He grinned. "Soon be retired."

She nodded. "I'll say goodnight, Eddie. Thanks for a lovely evening."

"No problem, princess."

"Will you call a cab?"

"No, it's only a fifteen-minute walk."

He leaned forward and kissed her again. She responded in a way she hoped showed neither keenness nor indifference.

A moment later, she waved him off and knew it was now probably between two and three more dates before things evolved.

"Text me when you're home safely," she called after him.

"Will do."

She closed the door. He'd be alright walking home late. His route was quite safe – two dozen streets of bungalows and semis.

She went to the kitchen to wash up the cups. It had been nice to eat authentic food. Back in her early twenties, she spent most of her money going out with friends. Eating out had been a big part of that because they loved going to restaurants, whether they be Indian, Chinese, Italian, or French.

Meeting Martin changed all that. He said saving for a house was more important, and he'd been right. But it had been no sacrifice for him at all.

She spotted a thin leaflet on the side – one that Ollie in HR had given her. She glanced at the opening paragraph.

> For some, retirement can trigger a loss of identity. You'll no longer be an administrator, plumber or driving instructor. This can lead to some people feeling less useful. Some will experience anxiety and depression, but they're not alone.

She stopped reading. This was hardly the boost her self-confidence needed.

A short while later, sitting up in bed with a magazine, she thought back to Martin again. That first time they met, he had an air about him, that he feared nothing. Then the last time she saw him just before his emergency heart surgery, he said he was a bit scared. She promised him, you'll be fine. But her promise meant nothing, and he wasn't fine.

A couple of magazine articles later, she was closing her eyes on a tiring day. She didn't want to grow old alone. She needed a bit of company. So, perhaps Eddie was the right man after all. He'd already texted saying he'd fought off a gang of giant green aliens to arrive home safely. He'd also asked for another date.

6

Choices, Choices

Sitting side-by-side in the conference room, Jo and Jennifer were waving at the screen and expressing their farewells to a client based in Germany. Three other Bonner's people were also waving from their kitchens or bedrooms as part of the Zoom call.

"Right, that's that," said Jo once the session had ended. "I'll update the schedule as discussed and circulate the new dates."

"Okey-dokey," said Jennifer prior to finishing off her glass of water.

They were halfway through Thursday morning with plenty to keep them occupied.

"Phew, it's so stuffy in here," Jo remarked as she gathered up her things.

"Hmmm, fancy a walk at lunchtime?"

"Yes, alright. Why not."

"I'll grab a sandwich from the bakers, and we can hit the park."

"Great. I was there yesterday and... well, I met some interesting people."

"Interesting? You mean weird?"

Jo recounted her chance meeting with a bunch of silly seniors dressed in daft costumes.

"They call themselves the Go Club."

"The Go Club? That sounds a bit racy."

"It's short for the Golden Oldies' Club," Jo explained.

"Ah, not so racy then. Still, it's nice to hear of people growing old disgracefully. That could be you next week, Jo."

They both laughed, although Jo was less than enthusiastic. It was okay though. She and Jennifer might soon be growing old *gracefully* – once a month over coffee and cake.

"Meanwhile," Jennifer continued, "I've got a fresh pack of double choc-chip cookies that needs opening."

Jo glanced at the wall clock. It was almost break time.

"I'll just wash my cup and pop over."

A few minutes later, they were relaxing with fresh coffee and cookies beside Jennifer's desk.

"Ready for the big send-off party?" said Annette, who was just finishing up working on something with Nina.

"Yes, it'll be nice," said Jo, taking it in her stride. Amid the usual ebb and flow, there had been a growing undercurrent of retirement party talk. Some seemed to be looking forward to it far more than she was.

"I love a party," said Nina.

You would – you're thirty.

"Me too," said Annette.

That was true. Annette didn't need an excuse. All those espresso coffees she lived on seemed to be part of an ongoing campaign to undo the damage of the night before.

"We'll all be there," said Kim. "It'll be good to get together just for you, Jo. I'm sure you won't miss coming to work."

Jo smiled and thought of Bessie all those years ago – back when an employer could legally throw you out when your time was up.

Poor Bessie.

"Oh well, I'd better be getting on…"

She finished her coffee and headed off to her desk in the other office. However, despite the work calendar being crammed full of activities, the past continued to paw at her.

She recalled joining Bonner's in her twenties, a few weeks after the firm had moved to Avalon House from Logan Place, a long since demolished Victorian courtyard. Back then, stories of the old premises were described with gusto by the original team, who seemed determined to make Avalon House newcomers feel like outsiders. Thankfully, that atmosphere gradually faded as the Logan Place originals changed companies or retired.

But now the boot was on the other foot. The firm was nearing the end of forty years at Avalon House, and for Jo it had become a second home.

"Got a minute?" It was Terry, her boss by the door.

"Yes, of course."

She followed him out to the corridor.

"All set?"

"For retirement? Yes, all set."

"We're going to miss you. No, *I'm* going to miss you. I rely on you, Jo. You're a legend in these parts."

"Thank you."

She knew she was blushing, but it felt good to be valued. And she certainly valued Terry's opinion. He was kind and considerate, and never one for drama. He was a boss you could take a problem to anytime and he'd help you find a way through it.

"Well," he said, "I just wanted to look you in the eye to make sure this is Jo Ramsey and not someone who's taken over her body. I'd better get back to it. I'm expecting a call. I'm sure you'll love it."

She watched him go and felt a surge rising in her chest. To have her loyalty to the firm appreciated so generously... it really was the most heart-warming feeling.

*

The Red Lion pub dated back to the 1920s. Inside, the cream and green décor with leather bar stools and dark wood furniture provided the ideal spot for drinks after work. Over the years, it had gone from an occasional thing, usually linked to someone's birthday, to a regular Thursday get-together. Jo always attended, although usually just for the first drink or two.

Of course, it was great chance for people to unwind, and some took full advantage of it – unwinding until closing time at eleven. Some continued to unwind on Friday mornings aided by paracetamol and coffee.

Topics of conversation were normally of the greatest imaginable variety – but not on this Thursday evening among the half dozen staff gathered around two tables pushed together in a corner. Despite Jo's best efforts, the conversation kept returning to one thing.

"That homeless people film looks like an interesting project," she said, referring to the early stages of a short animation in support of a national awareness campaign. "I can't imagine what it must be like to be out on the streets in all weathers."

"I like awareness campaigns," said Annette. "I wonder if anyone might commission one about retirement? Did you know forty-odd percent of the over-60s feel lonely? It's from an American survey. And it said two-thirds of them actually live with a partner."

Jo baulked. She hadn't asked Annette or anyone else to carry out research on her behalf.

"Just goes to show," said Kim, "you can't always look to the useless oaf you've married to be your retirement buddy."

"Yes, a retirement awareness campaign…" mused Amy, picking up her G&T.

Jo took a sip of her Sauvignon Blanc. It was good of them, but she had carried out plenty of her own research – including during that afternoon's tea break when she learned for the umpteenth time that one of retirement's big minuses was losing a work-based social life which could lead to the kind of loneliness Annette was referring to.

"Hobbies and interests," said Jennifer. "That's probably the way forward."

"What kind of hobbies and interests?" said Nina.

"Yoga?" Amy suggested.

"Meditation," said Annette.

"I'd take up judo," said Kim. "Or any martial arts really."

"Perhaps not," said Jo.

"A walk around Britain," suggested Amy. "Well, around a small part of it."

"You could save things from closing down," said Annette. "Libraries, cinemas… You could save them."

"Unusual languages," said Kim. "Ancient Sanskrit or something challenging like that."

"Klingon?" said Annette.

"You could hone your psychic side," said Amy.

Jo nodded and smiled.

"Pottery, perhaps," she said.

There was a general murmur of approval.

"That's probably the way to go," said Jennifer.

But that really was enough retirement talk for Jo. She was determined to switch back to work-based topics while she still could.

"There's another interesting project in the pipeline," she told Nina.

Nina took a sip of her drink.

"Workplace security in the cyber age," Jo continued.

"Volunteer for a good cause," said Jennifer, her focus still very much on retirement. "That's always a good idea."

"Absolutely," said Jo, not breaking eye contact with Nina. "This cyber security advice covers all the latest hacks."

"Good causes always need more people," said Amy.

"Well, more money, usually," said Annette.

"Which cause would you choose?" asked Kim.

Jo broke off her Nina-stare and shrugged.

"No idea," she said before turning back to Nina. "Can you believe some firms situated at street level have computer screens facing the windows? I wonder if Terry needs reminding before he sets up the new office space."

"Just think," said Kim. "You don't have to worry about any of that."

"Animals or children," Amy said. "I'd go around with a collection tin for those."

"It's not just the money though," said Nina. "Maybe Jo would like to work in an animal shelter?"

"If she's anything like me," said Amy, "she'll cry every day until she finally flips and brings all the strays home to live with her."

"She'd be in the local paper," said Annette. "Elderly woman living with a hundred cats and dogs."

Elderly?

"You could join a gym," said Kim.

"Or a book club," said Jennifer.

"Yes, I'm sure there are lots of opportunities," said Jo wishing James Bond would kick the pub door open and whisk her off in a getaway helicopter.

"I belong to a book club," said Kim.

"Yes, but you moan about it every month," said Amy.

"Only because we get an endless list of books I'd never pick. Most of them I don't read. I just go through other people's comments online and cobble together something out of that."

Jo didn't like the idea of reading books she had no interest in and then having to comment on them.

Amy scoffed. "I thought the point of reading was to broaden the mind."

Kim didn't like that. "It does broaden the mind – when they pick a book I like."

"Online discussion groups can broaden the mind," said Annette, although she was on the point of laughing.

"Yes," said Amy. "My cousin belonged to an online discussion group, until it got banned."

Jo waved it away. "I don't want to spend my time at home in front of a computer screen."

"What do you want to do then?" asked Jennifer.

Jo shrugged.

"Do you have many friends outside of work?" asked Nina.

"Yes," said Jo, meaning no.

"This isn't a very useful chat, is it?" said Amy.

But Jo wasn't so sure. It did seem to be a helpful exercise in ticking off all the things she wouldn't be doing.

"Couldn't you just stay on at work?" said Jennifer, almost as an afterthought.

But to Jo it wasn't an afterthought, it was a growing thought, but not in a helpful way. She was due to retire tomorrow.

7

This Is It

The hours were passing in a strange way, as if Jo were living outside of normal time. With retirement staring her in the face, each glance at the office clock felt like a farewell to that particular moment.

Goodbye 10:45 a.m.

Cheerio 12:17 p.m.

Toodle-oo three o'clock.

At 3:52 p.m., she was about to email a client regarding a draft contract. There was a degree of distraction though thanks to Jennifer waving from the doorway – not in a 'hello' way; more a 'come here' way.

Jo waved back in a 'hello' way and tried to immerse herself in the business of sending the email. But suddenly it was proving hard to concentrate. She was minutes away from completing forty years at Bonner's. Forty years of work, friendships, and having a purpose in life…

Ollie from HR squeezed by Jennifer and came over.

"Hiya, Jo. How's it going?"

"Oh, just finishing up."

"Just a bit of housekeeping to do on my part. Could I have your ID pass card and dongle?"

"Oh... yes... of course..."

She handed over the card – the one she flashed at whoever was on reception whenever she entered the building. And then she handed over the small black plastic dongle that she dobbed on the glass panel to raise the little barrier.

It felt like a court martial.

All the years, and months, and weeks, and days, and hours, and minutes had finally led to this – Friday 4 p.m.

"Everyone's waiting for you," said Jennifer.

They would be waiting in the canteen – so called because, for the first twenty years, a part-time catering assistant would serve tea, coffee, and savouries over the counter of the small kitchenette. These days, staff used it to eat their own sandwiches or catch up on reading or lost sleep.

"Jo?" Jennifer prompted.

"Yes..."

She deleted the email. It wasn't all that urgent. The client had only had the draft contract since last Friday. Someone else would no doubt follow it up next week. She thought for a moment about leaving a note on Amy's desk but dismissed it.

Instead, she closed the computer down, poured a little water into the aspidistra, and gathered up her things.

A few minutes later, Jennifer led her through the swing doors of the canteen on the sixth floor. Instantly, a cheer went up. At least thirty people were present; those from the offices she worked with along with a few from other parts of the business.

Jo gave a valiant smile as Amy stepped forward with a lovely bouquet of flowers and an envelope of Waitrose vouchers, while Annette, Kim and Nina handed out glasses of chilled prosecco.

The good wishes came thick and fast.

"Best of luck" … "It won't be the same without you" … "It's going to be a well-earned rest…"

She wouldn't cry, but tears felt very much on standby in case she changed her mind.

"To Jo!" announced Terry, raising his glass high.

"To Jo!" roared the gathering.

From somewhere, music filled the room – 'Jumpin' Jack Flash'…

"So how do you feel?" Amy asked, her voice raised above the Rolling Stones.

"Oh, I'm fine," Jo assured her. "There were nearly tears, but I rode it out."

"Any plans for next week?"

"Not as such. I thought I'd see where the wind blows me, so to speak."

"Very wise. It's good to give yourself time to settle into it. We'll have to get a few of us together once a month for lunch. You can keep us updated in person then."

Jo smiled. Those very words were an echo from an earlier time, said by someone else about another retiring colleague.

The next hour was a whirlwind round of chatting with her soon-to-be former colleagues. Buoyed by fizzy wine, she talked freely about the old days when she worked with Bessie, who took Jo under her wing. She also regaled listeners with her memories of Mr Bonner and her job interview, although she avoided any reference to the Logan Place originals, and how an unforgettable clerk called Victoria practically ran the company… and how, within five years of Jo joining, she was never mentioned again. No doubt, five years from now, newcomers at Skyline would tire quickly of stories about Avalon House. And as for Jo Ramsey? She'd be mentioned about as often as Bessie and Victoria.

At one point, Jo headed for the ladies' room thinking of the future. It would be great to have a whole new way of life filled with fun times and interesting challenges. Or was that the wine doing the thinking?

Two voices were coming from inside as she approached the half open door.

"Staying long?" one asked.

"Nah," said the other.

Jo held back for a few moments before entering. Inside, amid an atmosphere of stale disinfectant and freshly reapplied perfume, she was greeted by Annette and Kim who were just leaving.

"I'm thinking I might go for early retirement," said Kim. "Maybe we'll be retired together."

Jo laughed and thanked her but knew if Kim did leave, it would be to work for her brother-in-law's building supplies firm.

With Annette and Kim gone, she splashed her face with cold water and stared into the mirror.

This is actually it.

It seemed impossible.

And yet...

She splashed herself again.

A short while later, on her return to the canteen, she homed in on Jennifer.

"It's only a few months for you now."

"Yes, October. Not long to go."

Jo knew the details. Laurie, Jennifer's husband, would be sixty-six in October and qualify for the state pension.

But his generous head teacher's pension and income from two rental properties would mean Jennifer being able to join him despite being only sixty-one.

"We'll have to meet up for coffee," said Jo.

"Definitely."

"Perhaps a monthly thing."

"Yes, why not."

"Great. I'll look forward to it."

Nina came over.

"I can't stay – things to do. I just wanted to say best of luck for the future."

"Thank you," said Jo, "that's very kind."

"I've just been told I'll be standing in for you starting Monday, so that should be interesting."

"Perhaps I could give you a few pointers. There are a couple of projects…"

"No, honestly, it's just for the week until they sort something out, and I've got a meeting with the team on Monday to bring me up to speed."

"That's great. I'm sure you'll be fine."

"Thanks, Jo. Best of luck."

Jo watched her breeze through the exit. It was certainly a strange feeling. In forty years at Bonner's, she had never felt like a spare part before.

"A top-up, Jo?" It was Annette holding a bottle of bubbly against Jo's glass at an almost horizontal angle, which meant the liquid was flowing before Jo could respond.

"Thanks," she said belatedly.

But it was fine. She wasn't ready to leave her own party just yet.

The Beatles' hit, 'Help!' came on the small sound system. As a young schoolgirl, Jo had been a huge fan of the Fab Four – and now, after several glasses of fizz, singing it aloud suddenly seemed a good idea.

She wasn't alone.

The Diana Ross hit, 'Ain't No Mountain High Enough' followed, taking Jo straight to her teens and her first love.

More hits followed, as did more memories, and more prosecco.

'I'd Like To Teach The World To Sing.'

'Never Can Say Goodbye.'

'I Can See Clearly Now.'

"You're having fun," said Annette. "I've never seen you sing before."

"Yay retirement!" yelled Jo.

"Perhaps have some water," said Amy. She reached over to the table for a small bottle. She also put a couple of mini sausage rolls on a plate and handed it over.

"You're probably right," said Jo, accepting the offerings.

The music continued for another hour and Jo restricted her intake to two more glasses of fizz, making a total of... she couldn't remember.

Eventually, people began to leave in large numbers, each of them wishing her well. Several insisted she stay in touch, which was nice.

Finally, at ten past six, clutching her flowers and vouchers, Jo nodded to the waiting cleaner and left the building with Jennifer.

Outside, she breathed in the summer air.

"Are you okay?" Jennifer asked.

"Honestly, I'm fine."

She would pay for it though. She knew that. She hadn't had a hangover in decades, but one was most assuredly being lined up. She would no doubt wake up around four a.m. to discover her brain being bashed by the Hammer of

Virtue. And her tummy? That would have transformed into an industrial washing machine slowly churning the acidic Slurry of Justice.

"Well…" said Jennifer.

"Yes…"

They strolled across the almost empty car park. It really was a beautiful evening, but one Jo wasn't able to fully appreciate.

"Leaving Bonner's," she said. "It feels so strange."

Tears began to prick her eyes.

"Don't look back," said Jennifer.

So Jo didn't.

Not that it helped.

"You'll be fine," Jennifer assured her.

"I will. Tomorrow's Saturday. I've lived through plenty of those. And Sundays too. But Monday…"

She couldn't think of anything more to say.

"I'll say bye-bye then," said Jennifer.

"Yes, of course." Jo was well aware that Jennifer lived a bus ride away in the opposite direction. "Thanks for everything."

"Don't be daft. It's me who owes you. Keep well, Jo."

"You too, Jen."

For a few moments, she watched her friend walking away. Then Jennifer turned a corner.

And that was it.

All done.

8

Freedom for One

Jo stirred, gradually becoming aware of a growing expectation. For a moment nothing had changed. And then everything changed. After a Saturday hangover from all the alcohol and emotion, and a Sunday spent thinking about Monday, she had finally arrived at her destination.

It was now very definitely Monday at 7 a.m., and her alarm clock had as much on its morning to-do list as she did.

"Enjoying retirement?" she asked it.

Despite having nothing lined up for the next few hours, she got out of bed, donned her dressing gown, and opened the curtains on the new day.

"And so it begins…"

A short while later, at the table in the kitchen-diner, she worked her way through a bowl of oat flakes while the radio broadcast her regular classical music station. A glance at the wall clock told her it was a whole five minutes later than usual.

Wow, how the retired wallow in it.

After her cereal, she read a little more from the leaflet Ollie had given her, although she gave up after, 'stagnation in retirement can lead to difficulties with daily activities and a decline in mental health.'

Rising from her seat, she made a cup of tea and spent a few minutes checking the latest news stories on her phone.

Then, at the window, while she stared out at a whole lot of nothing going on in the garden, the radio show moved beyond the regular pre-work segments into a landscape of lesser-known features. Birthday requests. School run mentions. A daily quiz question...

When Jo did stir, it was to search for another radio station at random – the first time she had moved the dial in three years. As it was, her lucky dip turned up one dedicated to British and Irish folk music, which felt like stumbling across a secret room at Hogwarts.

After three songs, she re-tuned to her preferred station. *We can't have too much excitement in one day.*

To the tinkle of a Schubert piano impromptu, she went into the quiet, sunlit living room. Outside, the street was quiet.

Naturally, it would take a bit of effort to build a new kind of existence. She had friends at Bonner's, but now they would be mainly limited to social media. Yes, one or two would agree to meet her once a month for lunch, probably, but it wasn't going to fill her diary.

Up until last Friday, the future hadn't been something she'd given much thought to. But now a barren, unplanned expanse stretched ahead, and it wasn't good.

Oh, don't be so negative, Jo!

She turned away from the window. This wasn't the beginning of a jail sentence. It was more like being a kid at the start of the summer holidays. Except that instead of six weeks, it would last the rest of her days. So why didn't it feel brilliant?

"Be positive!" she urged herself.

She paced into the hall and back, muttering under her breath, "What to do, what to do…"

She stopped at the mantelpiece from where a myriad of faces stared back at her – most of them deceased family. She smiled at Mum, who looked forever radiant in a monochrome snap taken on Poole Quay in 1963. Alongside it was a photo of Martin and herself at a wedding in Bournemouth around the millennium.

What would he do?

She thought about that. To be fair, bless him, Martin would have done something dull. Perhaps she should do the opposite and go with something he wouldn't have considered in a million Mondays.

"Shopping!"

She hadn't planned to do any shopping, but surely that was the point. She would buy something. A new blouse or some summer shorts. Anything. The mall would be quieter than at the weekend – possibly even empty. She pictured it. Jo Ramsey alone in the mall. How would it feel? Nice and relaxed? Or like the beginning of an apocalypse movie?

*

She stepped off the half empty bus and squinted against the bright sunlight. On a Saturday morning, a horde of determined shoppers would have piled off with her, but today she was alone.

Strolling up the slope to the mall's glass-fronted entrance, she studied some of the poster ads – something she rarely did on account of not wishing to be trampled underfoot in the rush. But now, she could enjoy the advertisers' efforts and indeed was tempted, as suggested, to look at electricals on the upper floor.

Inside, she found the place almost deserted, which was no surprise. There were perhaps seven or eight people sprinkled around, and one of those was a uniformed cleaner wiping down a slatted chrome bench. Jo felt as if she belonged to a special club of mall 'insiders', smart and savvy, and free of the pain regular shoppers endured.

For a while, buoyed by the mall's relaxing background music, she enjoyed exploring her new world of leisure. There was no way back to the old world of work for her, so why not go in deep. And anyway, who wouldn't kill for this kind of freedom?

Gradually though, the place grew busier with older folk and mothers with toddlers in buggies. The overall vibe was still one of being wrapped in calm retail warmth, but now there was the occasional noisy complaint from a disgruntled child or pensioner.

Passing a coffee bar, she glanced inside. Four older people were seated at a table, laughing about something. One of them was eating chocolate cheesecake. Jo checked the mall clock. 9.45 a.m. It was like living in a parallel dimension.

Lifted by this new sense of being on a permanent holiday, she headed for one of the larger stores in search of a lightweight summer raincoat.

A short while later, she was trying one on – a waxy, sky blue, three-quarter length affair that seemed ready-made for the unpredictable British summer.

"Retirement is fine," she told herself. "Nothing to be afraid of."

She noticed a small boy by one of the long mirrors. He'd been studying his reflection but now he was watching her.

"Why are you talking to yourself?" he asked.

Jo spotted a woman on her phone in the next aisle – undoubtedly the boy's mother.

"Because I'm free," she told him as she took the raincoat off.

The boy's eyes widened.

"Did you escape from prison?"

"In a way, yes," said Jo, returning the coat to the rack.

Struck by a sudden terror, the boy fled, yelling, "Mum, Mum, that lady escaped from prison!"

A sales assistant stared at Jo from behind a nearby counter.

"Kids, eh?" Jo said with a grimace while turning and fleeing the store.

Twenty minutes later, she was seated in the quiet coffee bar she had passed earlier. The four elders had moved on to enjoy more of their day. In their place sat a golden oldie couple – probably mid-seventies and completely in tune with each other. Had they been married fifty years? Or had they only recently met? Or... was this a clandestine affair?

Jo sipped her latte. She had too much time on her hands, that was the problem. Her mind was beginning to wander. Although wasn't that a Miss Marple discipline? To sit invisibly and simply observe?

Mind. Wandering. Again.

"Freedom, lovely freedom," she said under her breath before taking another sip of coffee.

She picked her phone up and googled 'things to do in Tolcombe'. Encouragingly, there was something she could do this very lunchtime, should she choose.

She put her phone down again and glanced over at the counter, where she had bypassed the mouth-watering display of biscuits, cakes, and croissants. Maybe that had been a mistake.

A young man came in. To Jo, he looked like he might be a student. Once he'd taken a seat, she squinted to read the cover of his oversized paperback.

'Mathematical Methods for Physics and Engineering.'

The female waitress liked him. That much was obvious. At least it was obvious to Miss Jo Marple. But the student's nose was already in his book.

Ah well, the great love affair that never happened…

She considered it. While she was no expert in young love, it couldn't be said she had no experience of it. She recalled both instances.

Keith and Ty.

Staring into the foam on her drink, she chose to dwell on Ty. They were in a café one time. Where had that been?

Brighton?

Yes, Brighton. She would have been twenty.

She recalled them sitting there, nursing their coffees, the radio playing Roberta Flack's 'Killing Me Softly with His Song.'

Would she ever regain that feeling? That intensity? She could feel the hole in her being. The space. She was alive and alone.

She thought of Eddie.

Hmm.

Then she thought of Big Ben.

And there was that feeling again.

9

Things To Do

Following a shopping expedition that had resulted in zero take-home purchases, she was approaching a single-storey 1970s workshops behind the town hall. According to the blurb on the community activities page of the council's website, anyone could turn up and join in with the lunchtime sessions. The cost to working people was a tad on the pricey side, but the money was used to subsidize the cost to senior citizens.

Hopefully, pottery would be the first step to a fulfilling retirement. She had done some googling too. The potter's wheel was invented 7,000 years ago in Mesopotamia and there was earthenware, stoneware, and porcelain. Also, she had seen the movie 'Ghost' three times.

A dozen or so potters were active in the bright, sunny workspace when she entered. She hadn't signed up as yet. She just wanted to see what they got up to. But there was a definite air of purpose she liked.

"Hello," said a young male tutor. "I'm Aiden. Were you thinking of joining us?"

"Possibly. Is it difficult to learn?"

"Not really. You just need to give it a month or two. After that, it's all about practice."

Jo watched someone wrestling a fresh lump of clay.

"Would you like to try?" said Aiden.

"Um…"

Before she could decline, she was holding a small, cold, wet mass in her hands.

"That's right – just get the feel of it. And don't be afraid to give it a good squelch."

She did so but feared it might make a farting noise which she would have to pretend she hadn't heard. No doubt Annette from Bonner's would try for that kind of noise from the outset and roar with laughter about it.

Annette… unaware of being a replica of Chrissie who had talked and acted identically in the same space twenty-seven years before her.

"I've recently retired from work," she said, mainly because she felt awkward just standing there squeezing clay.

"That's great. We get quite a few retirees joining us."

"Like me," said a spindly silver-haired man in a Pink Floyd t-shirt and skinny jeans. "Are you loaded up with responsibilities? Or are you free like me?"

"Um…?"

"Take my advice. We spend our lives in school, in work, looking after families… you know the drill. Now it's our time. Am I right?"

"Er, yes… you're right."

Having finished squeezing the clay, Jo put it down on a workbench.

"We also do a two-hour evening class," said Aiden. "It's a great introduction to throwing on the wheel. You'll learn enough to make a basic bowl or cup, or you might go for a small planter. Either way, you'll have something to keep."

"You'll love it," said a lady with blue hair. "I've made hundreds of pieces."

Wiping her hands on a tissue, Jo struggled to visualise it. She'd had it in mind to put something small on the shelf by the front door, but now she was seeing her house full of wonky pots.

"I don't have a lot of room," she said.

"Some of us sell them for charity," said the elderly lady.

Ah, then someone's else's house gets filled with wonky pots.

"Possibly then," said Jo knowing she wouldn't be coming back. She would simply make a cash contribution to a local charity and save the town from a glut of abysmal ceramics.

As far as retirement went, this wasn't a great start.

*

Jo was enjoying a toasted cheese sandwich and a glass of fresh orange juice at a small café near the library. This was handy for two reasons. The toastie was delicious, and she was due at the library directly after lunch to meet a reading circle.

While she ate, she listened to the café's radio, which was tuned to a lunchtime request show. At least a dozen people had texted in their best wishes to hubbies, daughters, and all sorts. Jo thought of joining them under a false name. 'This is Henrietta in Cornwall wishing Jo Ramsey a happy retirement and saying how jealous I am.'

As for the reading group, Jo had seen a piece about them in the local paper at the weekend mentioning that newcomers were always welcome. She still wasn't overkeen on the idea of reading books she had no interest in, but she was balancing that with Amy's comment about how reading broadened the mind. She also couldn't help but think of Bessie retiring from Bonner's all those years ago, and how that turned out.

She sipped her orange juice. It was important to get retirement right.

*

It felt strange entering the library. She hadn't been inside since… she couldn't quite recall but suspected she might have been a teenager. Bookshops were her thing. She went into those three of four times a year, but the library – perhaps now she would become a regular.

The first thing she noticed was the smell of used books – or at least something of their essence merged with airborne dust and floor polish.

Over to one side, huge, dark, sturdy shelves housed Fiction A-O. In the middle of the floor, smaller bookcases provided a home for the remainder. On the other side of the large space, beyond the calm of the reference area, there was a mezzanine where people could have tea or coffee from a machine.

And there they sat, literally in a circle. Eight woman and two men with, she guessed, an average age of sixty-five.

These were her people.

She felt a pang of anxiety as she approached but smiled when challenged with a "hello?" from a sprightly woman with a white quiff and red neckerchief under a dark blue blazer.

"I saw an article in the local paper," Jo offered. "Is it alright if I sit quietly?"

"New members are always welcome. Please take a seat. I'm Pam."

"Thanks. I'm Jo."

She acknowledged the welcome from all sides, and yet...

At Bonner's, she mixed with an age range of twenty-somethings right through to those nearing retirement – a mix that represented the economically active society. This reading group represented something else. They were clearly decent people, good people, avid readers – and they probably didn't need half-hearted members, but...

"We're discussing the novel we've just finished," said Pam.

"Oh right," said Jo.

The man next to her showed her a paperback copy of the book. She squinted at the title: 'Heat Loss.'

She tried to conjure up the story. A hunky male plumber... a woman whose heating had packed up... but why was there a rugged coastal scene on the cover?

"So," said Pam, "let's wrap up our thoughts on Heartless, shall we?"

Heartless?

It was the curly writing. Why didn't book covers employ a nice simple font like ariel? Imagine the Rivers and Canals report a client sent over last week. Using curly writing, it might have looked like a report on Ravers and Camels.

She let the remainder of the discussion wash over her. Heartless sounded like a decent romance, but one to be read in private, not to be pored over in public. Thankfully, they were done within ten minutes, with a red-faced lady making the final comment that it contained far too much you-know-what.

"And now for the most exciting moment of the month," said Pam in much the way a TV game show host might tease the big prize. "It's Mary's turn to reveal our next book. Mary?"

"Thank you," said Mary. "I thought long and hard about this…"

To Jo, Mary seemed mouselike – the sort of person who wouldn't say boo to a three-year-old. So maybe she'd spent the last few weeks working out how not to disappoint everyone.

Mary held up a paperback.

"It's in the current Top Ten and it's called 'A Daughter's Dread'."

Jo tried to process the twelve-inch bloodied knife sticking out of a birthday cake.

"Ooh," said an elder member of the circle. "I don't like the look of that."

"It's a dark story," Mary stated unnecessarily. "A daughter suspects her mother of murdering the man next door. Will trying to uncover her mother's hidden past place her own life in peril?"

"Obviously, it's widely available," said Pam, clearly for Jo's benefit. "So, we all have plenty of time to get a copy and read it before our next meeting."

Jo nodded but knew she wouldn't be reading 'A Daughter's Dread' before the end of the month, nor indeed before the end of her time on Earth. Her next read would be something chosen by herself. Something heart-warming…

Twenty minutes later, she left with a smile and a vow to never return.

"Well, that's Monday almost over," she told herself as she headed for home.

This whole retirement business needed more thought, she decided. And more support too. She would contact Marilyn.

Her phone pinged.

It was a text from Eddie saying he was looking forward to seeing her tomorrow.

This made contacting Marilyn even more advisable. Perhaps, she could offer some advice.

10

The Bubble & Squeak Café

Mum's hand was a blur as she whisked eggs in a bowl. It was a good opportunity for young fingers to snake up to the choc chips on the plate…

Jo rolled over in bed, gradually losing touch with a receding dream and becoming more aware of morning peeping through a crack in the curtains.

"Yay, freedom…" she croaked.

It was her second day of retirement and time to strike a decisive note. She could do absolutely anything. How many people would love that opportunity? Okay, so they might prefer to be a few decades younger so that 'absolutely anything' would involve an actual range of choices…

She tossed aside the duvet and rose from her bed. Pulling on her dressing gown, she threw open the curtains to let in the day. The street out the front looked the same as ever.

"Watch out world, here I come," she whispered – although there wasn't much world to see apart from a ginger cat sitting in the middle of the quiet road.

A short while later, at the dining table, munching on oat flakes, she was listening to another random radio station – one that played lots of upbeat pop music to lift the mood, which was no bad thing.

After breakfast, she washed up her things then went upstairs for a shower. She followed this with a chapter of a gardening design book before deciding that she was ready to face the day.

"Okay, here's another quickfire quiz question for all you lovely listeners," said the radio presenter. "Are you ready?"

"No," said Jo, "I'm meeting Marilyn."

Switching the radio off, she wondered what the quickfire quiz question might have been. Perhaps it would have probed an important aspect of the human condition or challenged a political preconception. Then again, the previous question had been: 'Who won this year's Love Island?'

She paused before leaving the house. What was she hoping to get from seeing Marilyn? Did she really believe her friend could advise her on Eddie or retirement or anything else?

*

In glorious sunshine, Jo walked half the route to Bonner's before veering left and cutting across Tolcombe Park. She arrived at the Bubble & Squeak café to find Marilyn waiting by the door.

"Thanks for meeting me," said Jo. "I really appreciate it."

"It's a pleasure. How's it going?"

"So far, so good. It's Day Two and I'm not having conversations with the furniture yet."

"That's good. Shall we...?"

The welcoming pungent aroma of freshly brewed coffee hit them as they entered, as did the tempting selection of sweet treats. It didn't take too long to make their choices and they were soon comfortably seated, enjoying lattes and Danish pastries.

"Mmmmmm," Marilyn moaned over a mouthful of pastry, possibly a little too sensuously, "these are good... so good... too good... not good..."

They both laughed, but for Jo it brought back memories.

The Bubble & Squeak café had previously been Eamonn's Eatery, run by genial Irish couple Eamonn and Mary. Jo would come in a couple of times a week for a chatty, fun-filled lunch with Bonner's colleagues Tony, Chris, Don, and Tina. Don was an older co-worker with whom Jo made terrific friends over the course of seventeen years, while Tina was a TV enthusiast who dissected soaps and dramas with Jo for a decade and a half. It struck her how permanent Eamonn's Eatery had seemed, and how they had been an immortal group for a time.

"Might you try some hobbies?" Marilyn asked, putting her half-eaten pastry down and bringing Jo back to the present.

"I'm not sure if I'm a hobbies person," she said, leaving out any reference to having tried a pottery class and a reading group.

"Right... so how's it going with your chap?"

"Eddie? Oh, not too bad."

"Do the two of you get on well?"

Jo picked up her cup.

"I think so. I mean he's very nicely settled into retirement." But sipping coffee, she reflected on Eddie's direction of travel, intimacy-wise. "That said, what's your opinion of new relationships in later life?"

"I'm married, so I'm probably not the best person to ask. If it were me in your shoes though, I'd want someone who could occasionally excite me."

Jo didn't like to ask, 'in what way?'

"You know the sort of thing I mean," Marilyn continued. "A romantic break in Barcelona, dinner at a Michelin starred restaurant... even a surprise bunch of flowers occasionally. That wouldn't hurt him, would it?"

Er... which him?

For Jo, the problem was Eddie's assumption that they would have a physical relationship. For a seventy-three-year-old man, he had some unexpected traits. Of course, her understanding of older people probably needed updating.

"I hope you don't mind me asking, Marilyn, but how old is your husband?"

"Gavin's sixty-nine."

"And is he still...?"

"No. Not at all."

"Ah."

"Hellooooo!" came a call from someone entering the café.

Jo recognised some familiar faces.

A trap!

"I hope you don't mind," said Marilyn. "Coffee mornings and lunches aren't fixed. This week it's this morning and Friday lunchtime."

"No, of course not," said Jo, observing that Owen Tate, freed from the clock tower, was around six foot tall and carried barely any extra weight around his middle. His blue polo shirt over fawn cargo shorts gave the impression of a man at ease with life.

A few moments later, all seated together, Marilyn reintroduced everyone.

"Jo, you've met Ruth. She's something of a figurehead in our little group."

"Ah yes, the dragon."

"I've been called worse," said Ruth.

"Oh, sorry," said Jo, not wishing to offend someone who had to be in their mid-seventies. "I meant the costume, obviously."

Ruth smiled warmly. "Don't you worry about it. I was pulling your leg."

"You've also met Yvonne," said Marilyn.

"Yes, the pirate. Lovely to see you again."

Yvonne, possibly in her late-sixties, was wearing something more sensible for a larger woman on a warm June morning – a floaty, sleeveless, floral summer dress that showed off the tattoos on her upper arms. Unexpectedly, she cackled.

"What's a pirate's favourite letter of the alphabet?"

"Er…"

"Arrrrrrrrrrrrrrrrrrrrr!"

Jo was completely bamboozled. Marilyn simply groaned before continuing.

"And finally, we have Owen – who's occasionally known as Big Ben."

"Hi again," said Owen.

"Hi," said Jo, noting how the sunshine had brought out the freckles on his cheeks. She also detected a subtle trace of sandalwood aftershave wafting across the table.

"Can I just apologise again for crashing into you," he added.

"Honestly, there's no need." No need unless he wanted to do so by whisking her away for an early lunch. "I hope your costume wasn't damaged."

"No, no, all good."

"So, this is half the Go Club," said Ruth. "We're missing a few."

"Yes, we are," said Marilyn. "Sharon's not well, Delia didn't feel up to it, Ruth's husband Alan is busy, and Mandy and Mitch are spending the month at a friend's villa in Spain."

"Lucky Mandy and Mitch," said Jo.

"But what about you, Jo?" said Ruth. "How are you settling into retirement?"

"I'm taking it one step at a time," Jo reassured her.

"That's good then. It can sometimes be a challenge. Some of us can feel quite lonely."

"No, really, I've still got my work friends."

"That's lovely," said Ruth, "although paths can start to diverge once we're away from the day-to-day hustle and bustle."

"I appreciate that," said Jo, now absolutely certain this was a set-up, "but we're a pretty solid bunch."

"You're so lucky," said Yvonne. "What kind of things do you do together away from the office?"

"Oh, all kinds. Drinks after work on Thursdays. Really, all kinds of things."

"That's good," said Ruth. "I worked as a doctor's receptionist, and I don't mind admitting it took me a while to adjust."

"Me too," said Owen. "I struggled a bit at first. I went through all different kinds of emotions."

He must have picked up on Jo's uncertainty because he continued.

"You might be experiencing one of them right now – a sense of freedom that feels just a bit different."

Jo nodded a little. "Yes… like a twelve-year-old at the start of the summer holidays. Six weeks that feels like it's going to stretch into forever."

"That soon wears off," he said. "I hate to say it, but some people are left with anxiety and boredom. This is where the danger lurks. It's easy to fall into bad coping strategies. Drinking too much; that kind of thing."

"I'm sure I'll be fine," said Jo.

Thankfully, the conversation moved on and various other topics were covered, such as Yvonne's swollen feet, summer fashions for older people, funny animal videos on social media, the cost of living, and holidays abroad. After thirty minutes that simply flew by, they were touching on day trips.

"I ought to warn you," said Marilyn, "we do have the occasional rowdy day out. We steal my husband's old minibus."

"Gavin uses it for fishing expeditions with his friends," Ruth explained.

"We have to check it for dead fish when we use it," said Yvonne. "No, not really. It's a lovely old thing."

Just then, Owen rose from his seat.

"Right, well… sorry to be a party-pooper, but I've got things to do."

"His allotment," Yvonne half whispered.

"Ah," said Jo. For some reason she felt disappointed, but she quickly shook it off. "An allotment sounds a worthwhile interest."

"It's not for everyone," said Yvonne. "Some retirees feel lonely talking to plants."

"Plenty of nice people at my allotment," said Owen. "Bye for now… and lovely to meet you again, Jo."

No sooner had they waved him off, Yvonne was back onto Jo again.

"So, do you have much lined up this week?"

"A few things…"

But something was wrong. To be sitting there while Owen was just the other side of the window checking his phone. Yes, she was seeing Eddie later, but…

"Hobbies?" Yvonne ventured.

The need to do something flared up. But what? Obviously, she couldn't act like a hormonal teenager.

Could she?

She rose from her seat and collected her bag.

"It's been lovely, but I must dash. I'm sure I'll see you again soon."

She left them and headed outside. Owen was already twenty yards along the street.

In her mind, she ran up alongside him.

In reality, however…

Doubts arose.

What was she doing?

In her youth, she would have called after him, asking to meet up, like she had with Ty. But the long years since those days had robbed her of her nerve.

She came to a halt outside the Crusty Cob bakers, her throat dry, her heart pounding. For the past three years, she had lived as a widow. So far it had been a life of complete and utter decorum. It wasn't right to suddenly have a schoolgirl crush on someone at sixty-eight. Eddie was the sensible choice. She had known him for twenty years. He'd been a close friend of her husband, who trusted him utterly – even to the point of lending him his golf clubs, which said a lot.

Her phoned pinged.

It was an email from Ollie at Bonner's, which was unexpected.

Things got even stranger when she read it.

11

Living in the Moment

"Well, this is lovely," said Jo, trying to forget Ollie's email.

She was with Eddie at their 'usual' table in Giovanni's on another quiet night for the Italian restaurant.

"There's a nice little Greek place up the road," said Eddie. "I thought we might try it next time. It's worth having three or four regular haunts. It keeps them on their toes. Here, watch…"

As the waiter arrived with their drinks, Eddie stared hard at his menu.

"That other restaurant? You're right, it's top notch. They really look after us, don't they."

The waiter set out their drinks, smiled, and departed.

"I reckon that's free limoncellos later," said Eddie.

Sipping her gin and tonic, Jo enjoyed the icy blend of lime and botanicals.

"Mmm, that's very refreshing."

"You're doing well."

"Thanks."

"Making smart choices."

"Lime instead of lemon in gin and tonic, you mean?"

"Martin would be proud of you."

She wasn't sure what to make of that so, unusually for her, she gulped down some more or her drink.

While Eddie got started on ways to get the best out of life, Jo wondered about later. What tactics might he use? She also thought of the Go Club. Didn't they offer an alternative to Eddie?

"I had coffee with some new people this morning," she said. "They call themselves the Golden Oldies' Club. They seem a decent bunch… if a bit eccentric."

"Eccentric?"

"The first time I met them they were in the park wearing daft costumes."

"Oh, you don't wanna mix with cranks. Next thing you'll be transferring all your money to some weird cult."

"I'm sure they're harmless."

Eddie huffed and returned to his theme of getting the best out of life, but Jo wasn't listening. Instead, she studied the racks of wine and thought about widening her network.

"Does that make sense?" he asked.

Having missed whatever point he'd made, she nodded.

Perhaps she was overthinking things. Was it really Eddie versus the Go Club? She needed to calm down and engage her brain. Eddie wasn't all bad and she couldn't spend her evenings watching TV with Ruth and the others.

"…anything really."

She stared at him.

"Sorry, Eddie…?"

"Memories," he said. "Why don't you share some more memories?"

"Oh."

Why did he want to hear more of her memories? He hadn't listened to them last time. She supposed she could mention her son, William, leaving home to go to university. He was a forty-year-old finance director in Germany now. But Eddie had never had children. What if it were a sensitive subject?

"Meeting Martin," she said, playing it safe. "We were in our twenties, both working for the council. This was before he moved into insurance and I joined Bonner's. I was working as an admin temp and Martin was a deputy section head. One day he asked me to file some paperwork and we got chatting. It sort of went from there." She reflected on it. "It still seems strange not having him around."

"Yes, good ol' Martin, bless him," said Eddie, catching the waiter's eye.

"Yes sir. Are you ready to order?"

"Yes, garlic mushrooms and a chicken Caesar salad for me."

The sea of Italian names on the menu was formidable, but Jo wanted to try something different. The pressure was on though, so she quickly picked two items.

"I'll have the formaggio di capra and the ravioli tartufo, please." She had no real idea what to expect.

"Very good, signora. Thank you."

The waiter relieved them of the menus and departed.

"We're being a little adventurous, aren't we?" said Eddie.

"They were in the vegetarian section. I didn't want anything too heavy."

"Good thinking. I'm not a veggie myself, but I do my bit for the planet. You know there are people out there who just don't care. Not me though. I'm someone who cares."

"That's great, Eddie."

"I think it's important. If there was an injured dog right there by your leg, I'd be down there trying to help it."

Jo smiled as best she could, although somehow her appetite wasn't quite as keen as it had been.

*

Just before ten, they were back at Jo's place sipping coffee and dipping into a box of chocolate mints in the living room – yes, even Eddie.

"Told you, didn't I?" he said. "Free limoncellos."

"Yes, you did. It's a lovely way to round off a meal."

"It was a lovely meal with lovely company."

For some reason, her attention was drawn to the wallpaper. Too beige, too old, too faded. It needed updating. Perhaps something pale green or yellow or even monochrome with an accent of red?

"Have I told you how lovely you are?" said Eddie. "I mean you're right up there."

Jo smiled. On TV, people in their seventies were generally doting grandparents or bitter twisted failures who resented the young. Here was one acting like a lovelorn teenager.

"What's on your mind?" he asked.

"My mind…?"

"Go on, be as candid as you like. I promise I won't blush."

Jo guessed her thoughts probably wouldn't line up with his.

"Activities," she said.

His eyes lit up.

"What kind of activities?"

Uh-oh, danger.

"Ordinary activities. Hobbies and things. Pottery, reading groups…"

"Oh…"

"And perhaps making more friends."

"Why, are you planning to start an over-sixties football team?"

"I've been reading up on it."

"Football?"

"Retirement."

"Oh… fair enough, but don't forget life is all about living in the moment. Don't put things off. Seize the day. I'm speaking from experience. And I've read plenty of retirement literature too. Did you know you're at risk of being isolated and lonely?"

"Yes, I'm aware of the dangers. The advice I've been looking at suggests meeting different friends on different days and branching out to avoid getting trapped in a rut."

"If you're talking about joining the Golden Fogies' Club, I wouldn't bother. Friendship is about quality, not quantity. You need to be sensible about who you spend your life with."

Jo nodded, although Ollie's email had changed things – at least potentially. Two experienced people on the third floor at Avalon House had opted out of moving to Skyline, which would mean a shortage of knowledgeable individuals during an expansion of staff numbers. She wouldn't mention it to Eddie though.

"Look," he said, "you're one of the lucky ones. You should be doing cartwheels."

"I don't understand."

"You've got freedom, you're healthy, you've got some money in the bank, you're not responsible for looking after anyone…"

"Oh, I see."

"Jo, you've been blessed. I mean obviously there's a touch of boredom there, but you'll soon find your feet.

There's a ton of lists online about things to do in retirement. And more than that... well, let's just say you bring a good feeling into my life."

"Oh... well..."

"I know I'm getting on, but I hope that's okay. I've been on my own for a couple of years but I'm ready to love again."

"Love?" Jo's chest tightened.

"Yes, love. I want your retirement to be the happiest thing you've known since... well, since Martin left us."

Us?

He made it sound like a threesome.

"I want us to be together, Jo, and I know he's up there looking down and giving his blessing. I want us to be together for the rest of our lives."

"Right. Well... so... um... what kind of things are on those lists?"

"What?"

"The ton of lists online?"

"Oh, good things. Ideas. Visit a sacred site. That kind of thing."

"A sacred site?"

"Yes, Machu Picchu, kind of thing."

"Machu Picchu?"

"Yes, or book a show in New York, or read Fifty Shades of Grey, or become a stand-up comedian."

"Well..."

"Or there's playing the violin, knitting, photography..."

Eddie put his coffee down and moved in closer. His lips were quickly on hers, despite her holding onto her cup for dear life.

"We could do it all together," he whispered.

12

Art for Art's Sake

On a sparkling summer's morning, Jo was clearing out the garden shed. It had been a cluttered mess for too long, with spare garden chairs, plant pots, compost bags, garden tools, timber offcuts, decorator's sheets, tins of paint and who knew what else all jumbled up. She would get rid of everything that was no longer useful.

She gripped, she pulled, she yanked, she heaved – but in the rising heat, with sweat seeping into her t-shirt, it was harder than she'd foreseen.

Eventually though, she had everything spread on the lawn like a Turner Prize-seeking art installation – at which point she wondered why. Hadn't it all been safely stored out of sight in the shed?

No, things must go!

She surveyed her choices and plumped for a half-full plastic water bottle lurking on a shelf at the back. The best before date had passed two years before Martin.

Yuck…

Holding it at arm's length, she emptied the contents onto a rose bush, hoping no damage would be done.

Her phone rang. Pulling it from her pocket, she checked the screen. It was an unknown number.

"Hello?" she answered, ready to fend off anyone pretending to be from her bank or the police.

"Hello, Jo. It's Ruth. I got your number from Marilyn. I hope you don't mind."

"No, not at all. How are you, Ruth?"

Jo was worried that Ruth sounded a little breathless.

"Fine thanks. Just out for a walk in the park. I make sure I walk every day. It's the best thing we can do to stay fit and healthy, don't you think?"

"Yes, I do."

Jo wondered. Did the Golden Oldies' Club only attract the lonely? Okay, so perhaps it wasn't a membership requirement, but was the club a kind of substitute family?

"It's important to stay active," Ruth continued. "I walk, I do a bit in the garden… then, there's the Go Club, and Alan, my husband. He often surprises me with something or other."

Jo smiled. Eddie had failed to surprise her last night. His push for a bedroom encounter had been easy enough to deter. But she needed to make some big decisions about what she wanted from life, because repelling Eddie twice a week was hardly fair on either of them.

"Did I hear you're in a relationship?" Ruth asked.

The conversation suddenly felt odd – as if Ruth had all day.

Oh, she does. We both do.

Jo checked across the adjoining gardens to make sure she wasn't being overheard.

"I'm seeing someone but it's very early days. The same goes for retirement. I suppose I'm still finding my way. There's so much time to fill, isn't there."

"Yes, there is. Aside from walking and gardening, I do quite a bit of reading. Are you reading much at the moment?"

"No, but I intend to."

"I'm halfway through a book about first love in the 1960s. To be honest, I don't know if I'm enjoying it because of the story or because it takes me back to my own first time."

"Your own first love?"

"Yes… all those years ago."

Ruth seemed to drift off for a moment. Jo wondered what to do.

"Um, was it genuine love?"

Instantly, she wished she hadn't asked – but Ruth took it in her stride.

"I was a teenager. He took up all my thoughts. In my head, I planned a future, a family… I suppose we all go through it."

Jo hesitated, but it seemed rude to say nothing.

"Yes, it's a special time. For me, there was this intense day that ended in our first kiss. By then, I knew we'd be together forever."

"Ah, young love."

"His name was Keith and… well, after our day together, and the build-up to that kiss, my heart thumping, the kiss itself… he looked at me with his lovely blue eyes and said he and his family were emigrating to Canada."

"Oh my gosh. What a surprise."

"That's when I felt it. The love and the loss. He broke my heart. I mean really smashed it to pieces. I thought I'd never recover in a million years, but… well, they say young

79

hearts do mend. So, yes, I loved him. I thought the world of him. Then he was gone and I grew up. Last I heard he had a huge family and was a professor of physics."

"What times we have hidden away in our hearts, Jo. You must come to Delia's for lunch on Friday. I'll text you the details. You'll love Delia – she's so warm and friendly. And there'll be a few of us you know there. Yvonne, Marilyn, Owen…"

Owen…?

"Thanks, that's very kind. I'd love to come along."

"Great. See you Friday then."

After the call, Jo beheld her cluttered lawn. Seriously, what could she throw out? The odd pieces of timber might be useful for repair jobs. The decorator's sheets for painting. The spare garden chairs for a Go Club visit. All the other items… possibly useful in other circumstances?

She returned everything to the shed, padlocked it shut, and threw the empty plastic water bottle into the recycling box.

"Well, that's an hour of my life I'll never get back."

She wondered if this was more evidence of her being useless at retirement. It seemed so. But her thoughts were already on Friday. And Owen.

*

Jo was heading for an art class at Tolcombe Park Institute, home to various adult education classes and community activities. Painting for pleasure had featured in a TV mystery as the passion of one of the characters before she was brutally murdered. It had struck Jo as relaxing.

Reaching the campus, she spotted the art class already in action through a ground floor window across a patch of green. There were some older people at easels – one of them was a tall woman wearing a thick yellow Alice band to hold her hair back.

Stand aside, Rembrandt, here I come!

Of course, her long-departed paternal grandmother used to say art was for those who sought to avoid the responsibilities of real life. For a moment, Jo wondered if she might be about to confirm that analysis.

She entered the building's high-ceilinged entrance hall, which was refreshingly cool but surprisingly busy. Having already registered online, Jo tapped her code number into the reader and went through to the airy corridor, which would take her along to the class.

As she approached, she slowed a little. There was that same sense of trepidation she experienced before the pottery class and reading group.

But no – this needed to be pursued with gusto.

She peered through the half glass door onto a scene of quiet concentration. Then, with all the confidence she could muster, she pushed the door open and strode in.

The man's bare backside wasn't the first thing she noticed. That would have been the sketch of it on the nearest student's canvas. It triggered confusion in Jo's brain, with the only possible conclusion being that this artist was a joker, a prankster… until she turned her gaze in the same direction as his.

For a moment, she stared while trying to understand. Perhaps the human bottom was a metaphor for something.

"Are you looking for the beginner's class?" said a man entering the room.

"Er…?"

"This way."

A confused Jo followed him out, wondering if this sort of thing might lead to post-traumatic stress and flashbacks.

That was all she needed, images of a spotty backside disturbing her sleep.

"It's just in here," said the man, opening the door for her.

"Thank you… and sorry."

"Hello, welcome," said a lovely young woman as Jo came in. "I'm Catherine."

"Jo Ramsey, here for the beginner's class."

Yes, this was her place. Here, the students were painting still life in the form of a plate of fruit. She would never make it into an advanced art class. Not unless she went in as the life model.

Argh, the thought.

As Catherine helped her to set up beside the woman with the Alice band, she wondered why she had been so taken aback by a man's bottom.

Just get painting.

Once everything was in place, she was able to focus on the fruit. Except… what did those two apples placed together remind her of?

She needed a different piece of fruit to paint but would avoid the banana for fear of making matters worse.

Double standards. That's what her gran used to call it. Evil people who project a respectable image to hide hellish urges. Gran was born in 1900, a year before Queen Victoria died. She proudly called herself a Victorian baby, but teenage Jo only ever saw a Victorian adult.

After the class, she walked down to Tolcombe's vast natural harbour. It was such a beautiful day – good enough to take an outdoor table at a waterside restaurant. A little coffee and carrot cake, and boats coming and going in a leisurely fashion that matched her own. It was perfect.

While she sipped coffee, her brain flicked lazily through other possible hobbies that might last the rest of her life.

Photography.
Let's scratch that.
Learn to play the flute.
Probably not.
Metal detecting…

She thought of the past, as she seemed to do more and more these days. Metal detecting had been Bonner's colleague Don's hobby. Back then, during his seventeen years with the company, she got to know everything about him, from his daughter's educational progress to his countless weekends spent in damp fields detecting bottle tops and bits of wire. Two of the high points of his life were his daughter's graduation and the discovery of a small Saxon coin in West Sussex. He was the best male friend she ever had. They shared so many laughs. Then, around twenty years ago, he quit Bonner's to work for an international charity in the Middle East. Last she heard he'd retired to Norfolk and passed away a couple of years ago aged seventy-five.

Her phone pinged. It was another email from Ollie.

'I've now had a more detailed chat with Terry. He says he knows you'll be busy enjoying a wonderful and well-earned retirement, but if…'

Jo looked away from the screen. Out on the shimmering water, a huge white yacht was hosting a noisy drinks party.

But if…?

13

The Go Club at Delia's

Jo wasn't sure how long it would take to walk through the leafy streets of semis and bungalows to Delia's, so she allowed plenty of time – grateful for the shade provided by an abundance of mature trees. On the way, she wondered if her life was moving in the right direction, especially now that Terry was wondering if she might like to come back to Bonner's.

According to the email, this wasn't an open-ended invitation. With the company due to move to Skyline and a new Head of Department coming in, Terry needed her decision by the end of the month.

Obviously, she would need more details, but…

Arriving at Delia's ten minutes early, she thought of hanging around outside but was worried someone might think she was casing the joint.

She rang the bell.

A moment later, silver-haired Delia opened the door as far as the chain link security catch would allow.

"Hello?"

"Hello, Delia. It's Jo Ramsey. Marilyn and Ruth might have mentioned me?"

"What's the easiest way to de-bobble a cardigan?"

"Er…"

Delia released the catch and opened the door.

"Come in, Jo."

Jo stepped into a lovely, off-white hallway with oak laminate flooring.

"I used to have a special brush," said Delia, drawing attention to her pink cardigan. "No idea what happened to it. Do you have anything for it?"

At Bonner's, Jo had dealt with companies involved in clinical trials, cryptocurrency, and infrastructure funding. How to de-bobble a cardigan wasn't the sort of thing she'd ever given much thought to.

"I don't think so. Sorry."

"Hmmm… come through."

Jo followed her into a living room decorated with muted yellow wallpaper, a light brown carpet, and cream twin sofas. There were also family photos in chrome frames and a large burnt orange vase full of tall, decorative twigs. It felt warm and inviting.

"Marilyn said you have some eye problems."

"Yes, cataracts, uveitis, and glaucoma. I'm on four different types of eye drop. How are your eyes?"

"Er, fine."

From what Jo understood, Delia had ties to rural Wales and had been planning to retire there. But her husband's passing five years ago and ongoing eye problems had dampened her desire to make the move.

"Could you get things out for me, Jo?"

"Yes, of course. Um…?"

"Top left cupboard in the kitchen. There'll be six of us. And put the kettle on. No need for you and me to wait for the others. I'm gasping."

"Will do."

In an all-white kitchen with black worktops, Jo put the kettle on and got six red mugs with white polka dots from the cupboard along with a matching teapot. There were a couple of long French sticks and a pack of custard tarts on the breadboard. Getting the milk from the fridge, she spotted ham, cheese, cherry tomatoes, coleslaw, and two bottles of prosecco. Lunch would be good.

"Jo?" Delia was calling from the other room. "When you've made the tea, could you read a letter for me? Only I can't read small print."

"Yes, of course. Won't be a minute."

Jo spotted the envelope by the toaster. It had already been opened, so she removed the contents.

It was handwritten.

> Dear Delia,
> I trust you're well. Hopefully, you're not still hanging out with that over-aged headmistress, are you? There's only so much of Ruth's homespun advice a person can take.

Jo scanned quickly though the rest of the letter to find it signed by 'Hattie'. Deciding to read it to Delia before Ruth arrived, she put it in her pocket and finished making the tea.

"Here we are," she said as she brought two full mugs into the living room.

Delia meanwhile took an envelope from her bag.

"Yes, so if you could read this for me."

Ah…

This second letter was from Delia's bank offering her a new tax-efficient savings account. Not at all interested, Delia took it back from Jo and tore it in half.

The doorbell rang.

"Would you mind, Jo, please?"

"Of course."

She was soon answering the door to Ruth.

"You found it alright then," said the club's figurehead as she came in.

"Yes, no problem."

Ruth reached the living room doorway.

"Hello, Delia. How are the eyes?"

"Still misbehaving. How are you?"

"Oh, a touch of hip, hint of knee. Nothing to complain about."

"Would you like tea or coffee, Ruth?" Jo asked. "I've just made tea for Delia and me."

"Ooh lovely, but I'll make it. We can't have new friends doing all the work."

"Oh, right, well… there's plenty of tea in the pot or…"

"Come and sit down," Delia insisted. "You're a special guest today."

Jo did so.

"So how are you finding retirement?" Delia asked.

"It's going well," said Jo. "I've survived my first week."

"It's a big change from working, that's for sure. What kind of job did you have?"

"Admin at a marketing company. It was always busy with so many things going on."

Jo kept it to a few brief highlights, giving Delia a short overview of forty years at Bonner's. Before she had finished, Ruth was with them again, seated and sipping hot tea.

"Well, it sounds fascinating. Now, Ruth, I've had a letter from Hattie. I tried to read it but I can never make out her terrible spidery handwriting. Could you get it for me?"

Jo stood up. "I'll go."

"It's by the toaster."

"Right," said Jo, aware that she had already taken three steps towards the kitchen.

A few moments later, she returned waving the letter.

"Shall I read it?"

"Oh, okay," said Delia. "Why not."

"The handwriting's quite difficult, but…"

Jo skipped over the opening comments and regaled them with a series of mundane events. When she'd finished, Ruth laughed.

"That's unusual. Hattie, usually starts by being rude about me."

"Oh, does she…" Jo looked over the letter again. "Yes, I must have missed that bit."

"Hattie moved away," Delia explained. "She won't use a phone as she's hard of hearing. And she won't text as she doesn't have a mobile phone."

"So, she writes," said Ruth.

"Yes, in handwriting that nobody can read."

The doorbell rang again.

"I'll go," said Jo.

A moment later, she returned with Yvonne.

"Yoo-hoo all! I hope you've saved all the juicy gossip for me."

"There's tea in the pot," Ruth advised.

A few moments later they were all seated in the living room.

"I do miss Sharon coming along," said Yvonne. "She's such a good laugh."

"Sharon's quite ill," said Ruth for Jo's benefit. "It's quite serious."

"Ah…"

"We were talking about retirement," said Delia.

"Retirement," Yvonne echoed. "I had a very sudden kind of finish to my working life. I was in retail, so you never quite knew where you were, but yes… a strange time."

"I think Sharon put it best," said Ruth. "When she finished working as a teaching assistant it was like being in a car on a sunny highway when it runs out of fuel and comes to a halt."

Delia sighed. "Yes, just as the rain clouds close in. Next thing, you're on the side of the road watching everyone else go by."

"But we aren't stuck," said Ruth, eyeing Jo. "If we turn away from the road, we see there's a smaller trail. And when we go down it we find things we never knew were there. That's where you'll find us."

"We help each other," said Delia.

"Yes," said Yvonne, "although remember the old saying. You can lead a horse to water, but you can't make it think."

"I think me saying we help each other was more to the point," said Delia.

"Well, I've always believed that every one of us should do our best," Jo assured them, although the doorbell prevented her from expanding on the sentiment.

A moment later, Yvonne let Owen in.

"Hello all," he said with a little wave.

"It's our man," said Delia. "Poor Owen's been outnumbered this past week."

"There's tea in the pot," said Ruth.

A short while later, Owen was sitting opposite Jo with a hot drink.

"Been on the allotment?" Delia asked.

"Yes, I had quite a bit to do."

"It must have been sticky hot," said Yvonne. "I'm sweating just thinking about it."

"That's why I'm a bit late. Had to pop home for a shower."

Delia nudged Jo. "Owen sings opera in the shower."

Jo tried to picture it. Owen. In the shower. Singing.

Stop it.

She then wondered how Delia knew.

"So, Jo," said Owen, "how's it going?"

"Oh fine."

"Would you say you had any passions?" he asked.

Jo took a moment. "You mean hobby-wise?"

"Yes, you know – books, travel, local history, that kind of thing."

"I've not really developed any passions as yet."

"What are you doing tomorrow?" he asked.

"Er… well…"

She was a little taken aback. Was he asking her on a date? She forced her face into a strained smile, although guessed he might think she was releasing gas.

"If you're not sure," he said, "try adding some structure. It helped me."

"Structure?"

Jo was confused.

Owen nodded. "When someone asks what you're doing tomorrow, it's empowering for you to know."

"Oh, I see. Yes. Structure."

The doorbell signalled another arrival and, before long, Marilyn was with them, seated with a cuppa.

"It's mainly retirement talk," said Ruth, updating her.

"Ah right."

"I loved my job," said Delia. "I definitely would have stayed on for a bit longer given the choice."

"You're seventy-two," said Yvonne. "I don't think NASA would be right for you now, eyesight or no eyesight."

"I worked at the airport in admin, as you well know."

"Just kidding, Delia. You know how much I care about you, and I'm happy to say in public that I do not hold you responsible for that time I went to Sweden and my luggage went to Mexico."

Delia did her best to look stern but broke into a smile all the same.

"As you well know, Yvonne, I loved being at work."

"I know you did."

Jo found herself nodding sympathetically.

"How about you, Jo?" Yvonne asked. "Are you sorry you've left the land of the living?"

"No, not sorry. I chose to retire. For me, it can't be dismissed after a week."

"It's not always easy," said Marilyn. "You had a work routine that kept you busy."

"I do have a calendar," said Jo. "It doesn't have many entries yet, but…"

"You'll get there," said Ruth. "There's plenty of literature to read too."

Yvonne smiled thinly. "Yes, although most of the literature advises staying fit. It asks if you've recently run to catch a bus or train and found yourself gasping and near to collapse. Don't these people realise if you leave home early, you don't have to run?"

"My son's forty," said Delia. "I don't think he could run for a bus. Not that he uses buses. Not with that Land Rover of his."

"I walk as much as possible," said Jo.

"Me too," said Yvonne. "And my health's not been too bad, touch wood."

Jo stayed out of it. Yvonne didn't need the newcomer to suggest that carrying extra weight in later life might lead to a greater risk of diabetes. Bonner's had made a short film about that for a private health clinic.

"I do sometimes wish I could go back in time though," said Yvonne. "Forty was a good age. I felt great and did everything I wanted. In fact, we had a fancy-dress party for my fortieth. I went as a pirate."

"You always go as a pirate," Delia pointed out.

"It's my lucky outfit. At my fortieth, I met a guy who was also dressed as a pirate. And guess what – by the end of the night, I got my hands on his buried treasure, yo-ho-ho."

"Too much information," said Delia.

"I was very active at forty," Yvonne continued. "I still would be given half a chance."

"Yes, well," said Ruth, "I remember forty being a good age *health-wise* too."

Jo recalled her own fortieth birthday but opted not to share. It was a day to remember, a night to forget. At least three of her birthday cards featured a Zimmer frame which, ironically, after a boozy night, would have come in handy. That was twenty-eight years ago. Twenty… eight. It seemed impossible.

"How about you, Owen?" Yvonne asked.

"Forty? That was a different life. Right now I'm a hundred percent committed to having the best retirement I can."

Jo was curious.

"What does that entail?"

"It's a whole range of things, but if I can give one tip – avoid anyone who isn't on the same level as you, commitment-wise. It took me a while to adjust, but I was lucky. I mixed with positive people who were determined to make a real go of it. I'd be wary of anyone who didn't share that view. That's why I love this club. Everyone's doing their best to make it work for all of us."

Jo nodded her approval. But was she as committed to retirement as Owen? Because if she wasn't, it would be impossible to get closer to him.

But that was okay. Wasn't it?

14

The Aspidistra Has Gone

Lunch at Delia's had left Jo feeling both happy and confused, mainly because she continued to lack focus and commitment when it came to retirement. The other post-lunch thought was that a thirty-minute nap on the bed might be in order. Her eyelids were as heavy as sandbags.

Before going upstairs, she wrote a brief email to Ollie. She really needed a few more details about coming back.

Just as she hit 'send', the doorbell rang.

A moment later, she was surprised to find Eddie on the doorstep without an invite.

"Hello, love. Alright for a coffee?"

"I wasn't expecting you," she said, her need of sleep taking flight.

"All part of the fun of being retired. We're not bound by boring timetables, are we."

She showed him through to the kitchen-diner where she sat him down at the table and made him a hot drink.

"You got anything in the fridge? I missed lunch."

"Doesn't the pub do food?" she asked, by now all too aware of the alcohol on his breath.

"Fair point, but I met an old mate and we got talking." Jo sighed.

"There's sliced bread in the freezer and cheese in the fridge."

"Cheese toasties, lovely. Thanks."

"I was thinking of a cheese sandwich and you making it yourself. However…"

She didn't want him drunk in charge of a grill pan.

"Do you like puzzles?" he asked as she set about making his late lunch

"Yes, I suppose so."

"Jigsaw puzzles?"

"Yes, there's one in the cupboard under the stairs."

"Animals?"

"No, fishing boats. Lots of whites and blues."

"Lovely."

"It is."

"Do you know what? We'll be great together."

"Yes, well…"

"Are there any old movies on TV?"

"No idea, Eddie."

"If you get one of those subscription services, you can watch thousands of 'em."

"Hmm…"

Twenty minutes later, with Eddie fed and watered and snoring on the sofa, she texted Jennifer at Bonner's asking if it was convenient to discuss a confidential matter.

Jennifer texted back. '5 mins.'

Jo stood in the living room doorway watching Eddie. He sounded like a diesel truck stuck in mud.

Her phone rang.

"Thanks for getting back to me," Jo began as she relocated to the kitchen-diner, "and I'm sorry to bother you at work."

"It's no bother at all. I'm in the car park and the sunshine's lovely."

"How are things there?"

"Well, you know most of the projects in the pipeline. I can't really say any more than that."

"No, of course not." Jo was naturally aware of the non-disclosure agreements all staff were obliged to sign.

"We had a new enquiry this week though. A group of scientists looking at ways to decrease ocean acidity."

"Wow, interesting."

"But that's not why you got in touch."

"No…" Jo took a seat at the table. "It's just that Terry was thinking I might want to come back."

"Oh? And do you?"

"I'm not sure. I was hoping Ollie would send me a few details of what Terry had in mind."

"Couldn't you call Terry? Or Ollie?"

"I know I can rely on you, Jen. Are you sure you haven't heard anything?"

"No, nothing. Is retirement that bad?"

"No, not at all. It's great to have so many potential ways to go."

"So, why come back?"

"I don't know. I suppose after forty years…"

"You mean it's what you know."

"Something like that."

"And you're not put off by the commute to Skyline?"

Jo rose from her seat.

"Millions of people commute every day. I'll just have to put up with it."

"I must admit it's strange not having you here."

"Thanks Jen, it does feel strange to think of my old seat there, empty and unused."

"Ah… not sure where your seat went, but they've pushed your desk against the wall to make more space."

"Oh… I suppose it makes sense. What about the aspidistra? Have they moved that too?"

"Last time I looked out of the side window it was sticking out of a skip."

"What? Oh well, I don't suppose they'd want to take it to the new place."

"No, I suppose not."

Jo peered through the window into the garden.

"So, you've heard nothing about me coming back then?"

"No, nothing official."

Official?

"How do you mean, official."

"Okay, cards on the table time. I did hear Kim talking to Terry about taking over your old job. That's it. I didn't hear anything about you coming back."

"When was this?"

"This morning."

"Ah… so they might have wanted me, but now Kim's stepped in."

"That would be putting two and two together, but from what you've said, then it's likely that's the situation."

"So, I probably won't be coming back then."

"I'm really not the one to confirm or deny it."

"Oh well, you'll be out of there soon. How long is it? Two months?"

"Not exactly. I'm staying on for an extra year."

"Oh?"

"Fact is, hubby and I have had a change of plan. We've decided to retire to Portugal."

"Portugal?" Jo was stunned.

"We go there on holiday twice a year, so it makes sense."

"Right, so… why stay on for another year?"

"We've only just decided, so it makes sense to start a proper investigation into where we want to live, property prices, selling our place, whatever else. We might as well have another year of full income while we sort everything out. It all adds to our pension pot."

Jo tried to be upbeat.

"Well, that's fantastic. It sounds like you've got everything sorted."

Which is more than some of us can say.

"Yes, so I get to work at Skyline. I can't say that part of it appeals."

"No… so how will you get there?"

"With hubby. He works in Bournemouth, remember?"

"Er, yes, so he does."

"It's only a fifteen-minute detour for him to drop me off."

"Well, fab. Well done you two. We'll have to meet up soon."

"Yes, we will."

"Okay… well… bye for now then, Jen."

"Yes, okay, by-ee."

Jo ended the call and thought of Jennifer and husband Laurie by a pool in Portugal. But the image broke up under the weight of Eddie's snoring. She came back from the kitchen-diner to check on him. It wasn't every day she witnessed a warthog on the sofa.

Back in the hall, she faced herself in the full-length mirror by the door.

So, what's the plan?

She almost laughed.

Plan?

One minute she was trying to be successfully retired, the next she was hoping to get back to Bonner's. And now…? In terms of retirement, she was nowhere. As for Bonner's – her desk had been shunted aside and her aspidistra was in a rubbish skip.

Workplace friendships? Yes, they were great with almost non-stop interaction. But once you'd left? Would you see them more than once a year? Most likely you'd be reduced to liking photos of their holidays on Facebook.

Her phone pinged.

It was an email from Ollie. 'No news yet.'

"Oh Ollie, you liar!"

"Uh?" groaned Eddie from the living room. "You okay, Jo?"

"It's nothing. Go back to sleep."

"You couldn't make me a cup of tea, could you?"

Jo stared at herself in the mirror. Was this it? At sixty-eight, should she simply be grateful that a living, breathing, snoring human needed her? Was her role now to be there for Eddie despite having no love for him? To be satisfied because she wouldn't be alone? To say whoopee, Eddie wants some tea or dinner or a fumble in the bedroom? What about Jo Ramsey, the person, the dreamer of dreams?

She felt drained and lost.

"Jo?" Eddie enquired from the sofa.

"Not now, Eddie." She tried to think of an escape route. And then it came to her. "The aspidistra's gone."

*

A few puffy white clouds kept most of the sun at bay during Jo's power walk to Avalon House, so she avoided sweating too much. The journey itself was uneventful, although it was interesting to encounter all the familiar vistas once more. She had only been away a week, but it felt so much longer.

Crossing the footbridge, she slowed to appreciate the boats below. Maybe that was something to consider. Instead of being alone in her house, she could be alone on a boat.

She continued onward, over the main road, into the commercial sector, across the car park and up to the entrance. She paused. There was chewing gum stuck to the first step. And, over there, a KitKat wrapper.

Avalon House…

She gathered her wits and made for the side of the building where deliveries and rubbish were collected. There, as anticipated, sat a bright yellow dumpster full of unwanted office items. Topmost were a broken swivel chair, a dented drawer cabinet, the remains of a small partition wall, and a large potted plant.

"Good grief, how could they?"

Thankfully, it looked intact. However, she couldn't reach it, which left her with a clear alternative. She began to climb…

"Hey!" yelled an agency security man, who must have seen her approach the front door and then slip around the side.

Ordinarily, Jo would have engaged with him, but he was new and looked annoyed.

"What the hell are you playing at?" he demanded.

"I left this behind when I retired after forty years. I'm going to take it with me and give everything I can to making a go of it."

"You're not to take Bonner's property."

Jo bristled. "My friend Don bought this for me when he left the company. It's almost twenty years old."

The guard seemed less certain of both himself and the situation.

"Well, just take it and go."

She tried to. Except it weighed a ton.

"You couldn't give me a hand with it to the bus stop, could you?"

Clearly eager to get rid of her, he obliged.

15

Plotting and Planning

The Pirates of the Caribbean main theme blared from the radio in Jo's kitchen-diner, reminding her of Yvonne finding buried treasure. It brought a smile to her face.

It was just after ten o'clock on Monday morning and there was little to do – a.k.a. nothing to do. Worse still, having had oat flakes for breakfast at eight, she now fancied a chocolate hobnob with her coffee. But that wasn't right.

"Hobnobs are for eleven o'clock," she told herself. "That's why it's called elevenses. You can't have tensies."

She thought about that.

"Actually, you can."

Biting into a hobnob, she thought of Eddie – but the Pirates theme gave way to Pavarotti and Nessun Dorma, so she thought of Owen singing in the shower.

Stop it.

She shifted her focus to the vase of red roses in the middle of the table – a gift Eddie had sent over on Saturday with a note apologising for turning up unannounced and asking if she was free for lunch on Wednesday.

Finishing off her hobnob, she wandered into the living room. Over by the window, the rescued aspidistra looked nicely at home. At least that was something sorted. After a weekend devoid of company, her retirement was... not boring, because that word had been banned. No, her retirement was... in need of help.

Her options to fix the situation seemed to boil down to contemplating some straightforward questions and some not-so-straightforward answers.

Was she enjoying retirement?

Next question.

Did she want to live alone?

Um...

Did she want to live with Eddie?

No.

Was a relationship with Owen at all likely?

No.

Did she want to try out different partners via internet dating?

Nightmare alert!

She returned to the kitchen-diner where she fired up her laptop. At Bonner's, her work calendar had always been crammed full. It was time to fill her retirement calendar likewise. From now on, life would be action packed.

She stared at the screen.

Hmm...

If her work calendar had been a rainforest bursting with life, this was the Gobi Desert, empty and barren. She had to fill it somehow though... or at least place a single oasis in there somewhere.

Coffee with Marilyn?

She jotted it on a post-it and stuck it to the edge of the screen.

Now what?

Her gaze wandered to the roses.

"Okay…"

She typed in an entry for Wednesday. 'Lunch with Eddie.'

Eddie…

He had made her think about cookery. Okay, so that was probably because he wanted an in-house chef, but he had inadvertently opened a door.

A memory came back to her.

Sixty years ago…

Mum's hand… a blur as she whisked eggs… and a young hand surreptitiously snaking up to the chocolate chips on the plate…

Although Jo was only ten when she lost her mum, she remembered their kitchen sessions well. It would have been the early 1960s. Mum's special brownies came to mind – a crispy top over a soft fudge middle. She could hear Mum's words, how it was vital to cream the butter and sugar before adding the eggs, which in turn required… "mixing to death or ten minutes, whichever comes first." Jo recalled why – because it aerated the mixture, which is what gave the finished brownies a crispy top.

Mum was always baking and cooking and singing and laughing. Then, with Mum gone, and Dad busy working long hours, Gran took over and it stopped. Suddenly, for Jo, the house was quiet and the focus was on 'improvement' and 'standards'.

"Right," she said, ripping the post-it from the edge of the screen and screwing it up.

She grabbed her phone and made a call.

"Marilyn, hi, it's Jo. I was thinking about doing something for charity. Do you have any ideas or advice?"

"Hello, Jo. That's quite a big topic. We could meet if you like?"

"Oh brilliant, thank you. Is it too bold of me to suggest lunch today?"

"Today? Okay, where shall we meet?"

A few moments later, Jo was typing an entry into Monday on her retirement calendar.

'Lunch with Marilyn at Bubble & Squeak.'

*

Over cheese toasties and a glass of prosecco, they caught up with each other's news. It was great fun and a much-needed boost to Jo's self-esteem.

"I'll be a write-off this afternoon," said Marilyn. "A definite snooze fest."

Jo laughed. "I don't mind the occasional nap myself."

"To doze or not to doze? You must get it right though. I've read up on afternoon naps and there's a lot of conflicting advice. Thirty minutes is perfect, but don't sleep for an hour as that leads to diabetes… but do sleep for ninety minutes, as that means you get a full sleep cycle."

Jo nodded. "That's as clear as mud."

"My advice is close eyes, dream about a romantic encounter, open eyes, drink tea."

"At last, some sensible guidance."

They continued chatting and having fun all through their toasties, a fruit salad, and two glasses of prosecco. Then Marilyn surprised Jo.

"Can I ask you something? Is there anything between you and Owen?"

"No," said Jo without hesitation. "Why do you ask?"

"Oh, no reason. I just saw the way you… as I say, it's nothing. And it's certainly none of my business."

"I do like him, but I'm not sure we have much in common."

"For what it's worth, I think women should go after what they want. Men don't give up unless it's lacking in their DNA to start with."

Jo sensed a little of Marilyn's personal life in that last comment, so she changed the subject.

"How about we discuss the reason I called you in the first place. Do you think I could do a charity thing?"

"Possibly. What did you have in mind?"

"I'm not sure. I was thinking maybe something the Go Club could join in with?"

"I'm sure we'd be happy to support you. Basically, you're looking for something that's fun to do but doesn't require us to put our hands too deeply in our pockets."

"That's a fair point."

"Sharon set up the walk we're doing. That's kind of our level."

"Ah yes, the funny costumes."

"It's to support a fund that supplies toys to children in hospital."

"Oh, what a lovely idea."

"The walk's probably a bit too soon for you, fitness-wise, but I could forward you the email."

"Thanks."

But was it a bit too soon? Should she join them in doing the walk anyway, fit or not? Although… what if she conked out and they had to carry her? No, she'd think about it before making a promise she couldn't keep.

"Is Alan a club member?" she asked. "I haven't seen anything of him."

"Yes, he's a member, but he prefers to let Ruth get on with it."

"Oh right. So, what line of work was he in?"

"You know the big cruise liners? He worked in the sales office. Nowadays, he plays crown green bowls."

Marilyn's phone rang.

"Excuse me a moment," she said as she took the call.

There followed a minute of back and forth before she ended it.

"Something's come up," she said. "My daughter needs an emergency babysitter tonight."

"Oh lovely."

"Yes, little Rosie is four and a treasure. But it means a heck of a journey to Lymington."

"Oh well."

"Thing is, I'm due to give Owen a hand with Yvonne this evening. She's struggling with attending her weight loss class. Would you be okay to take my place?"

16

Seriously, Yvonne

Jo was with Owen at Yvonne's place, the ground floor half of a Victorian terraced house not far from the park. Standing in the hallway, Yvonne was dressed in cut down denim shorts and a black baggy T-shirt. She didn't seem in a hurry to go anywhere. Meanwhile, peering into the living room, Jo was surprised by Yvonne's interior design choices.

"How… abstract," she noted, referring to the art on canvasses hanging on the walls.

"What do you think? Brilliant or terrible?"

"Um…" It was hard to be sure either way.

"Honestly, you're free to say they're terrible… as long as you don't mind watching a grown woman curl up into a ball and cry for two hours."

"They're amazing."

"Oh thanks. I've been painting since I was six," Yvonne explained with pride.

"Such creativity," said Jo, deciding to avoid mentioning her own failed foray into creating art.

"Are you a fan of abstract expressionism?"

"Er... well, I like these. Especially the one over the fireplace. That's lovely."

"There's a story behind that one..."

"Shall we get going?" Owen suggested.

"Right," said Yvonne, clapping her hands together. "I'll just go and change my life... sorry, clothes! Then we'll whiz off down there."

"No worries," said Owen. "You have an entire three minutes."

"Honestly, I won't need half that. Why don't you two take a seat."

She was indicating the living room, but Owen held his ground in the hallway.

"I'll wait here. Jo will wait by your bedroom door."

"You don't trust me."

"Don't be daft," said Owen. "Now how about you choose what to wear?"

Yvonne strode off down the longish hallway and into a room on the right. Jo followed and paused outside.

"Won't be long," Yvonne called from behind the half-closed door.

"I think that's the general idea," said Jo.

"Do you know something," Yvonne mused, "I thought about being loved by someone today. I was having a light salad lunch and that popped into my head. How weird. Do you think it was the pine nuts?"

"Um... you *are* getting changed, Yvonne?"

"Do you think being sixty-eight is a problem?"

"We're the same age. I'm sure it's not."

At least I hope it's not.

"If I could attract a man, do you think bedtime would be more about cocoa than cuddles?"

"I'm honestly not sure."

"I hope you're not shocked by the word cuddles?"

Jo glanced at her watch.

"No, I've heard far ruder."

"I should probably join a gym," said Yvonne.

"I'm sure the weight loss meetings are more user-friendly."

"True… except Milly will be there, no doubt revealing chapter 287 of Milly's Life of Woe. Last week she said having your husband walk out is the ultimate betrayal of a woman. I said what about the time my local restaurant ran out of chocolate dessert?"

A phone beeped.

"It's WhatsApp. Milly's asking if I'm coming tonight. She's lost two pounds."

"Yvonne, you're not in competition with her."

"It's okay, I'm typing something positive."

"Great."

"Of course I have no idea if I've lost any weight this week. I refuse to use my scales. They're too spiteful."

"Well, it's none of my business."

"No, it's okay. It's better that I talk about it."

"Okay, as long as you talk while you're dressing. Do you have targets?"

"Yes, an annual one."

"And have you managed to lose anything?"

"Yes – my mind."

"Seriously, Yvonne."

"Okay, seriously – I've lost thirty pounds."

"Seriously?"

"No, but don't worry, I'll definitely lose some weight by the end of the year – fingers, toes, and eyes crossed!"

"When I worked at Bonner's, the team did a campaign for a private health provider promoting simple exercise."

Silence.

"Yvonne?"

"It's okay, I've seen and read every piece of advice and I know I'm on the precipice of five hundred serious diseases."

"Yes, well, how are we doing in there? Almost ready?"

"Have you ever been on a blind date?"

"No."

"I went on one once. A friend set it up. I can't tell you how much I prayed for good luck"

"How did it go?"

"We got married and had eight children. No, hang on, we had a quiet meal and never saw each other again."

"Oh."

"It wasn't a surprise. The only thing we had in common was a complete lack of interest in each other's interests."

"Right."

"Take music for instance. I said I liked classical music. He said he preferred jazz. I said I'd prefer being eaten by sharks to an evening of jazz."

Something occurred to Jo.

"I like classical music."

"Maybe I should have dated you."

Owen coughed from the front door.

"Time to go," he called.

"Coming, honey-bunch," Yvonne called in a sing-song voice.

The bedroom door swung open.

"Ready," she said. She was wearing a floaty purple blouse over a floaty pink summer skirt.

"Perfect," said Jo.

"Are you sure I can't tempt you to a glass of wine? We could order pizza and watch some TV?"

"I think we're out of time."

They joined Owen by the front door.

"I do seriously want to get fitter and lose weight," said Yvonne. "Did anyone bring a car?"

"The walk will do you good," said Owen.

"Ouch."

On the way, Yvonne pointed out a nice pub. Apparently, it had been redecorated and would be worth checking out.

"Another time," said Owen.

"Then tell me about your chap, Jo. What's his name again?"

"Eddie, but he's more a friend than anything."

"Tell me more over a glass of wine."

Both Owen and Jo ignored her.

"Do you realise we're missing a really good cookery show on TV?" said Yvonne.

"I love cookery shows," said Jo.

"Really? Do you cook?"

"Not much, no."

"Don't you find it strange to watch cookery shows without trying the recipes?"

"Not really, Yvonne. I also watch detective shows, but I've never investigated a murder."

"Fair point, but life is full of surprises – like the whistling solo in Hey Jude."

Jo frowned. "There isn't a whistling solo in Hey Jude."

"Oh, it must have been me then."

Before long they were outside a 1950s church hall, waving her off.

"Thank you, guys," she called as she disappeared inside.

"Right, that's that," said Owen. "Thanks for coming."

"No problem at all."

"I'm happy to help Yvonne but there are times she won't come out of her bedroom."

"As I said, I'm happy to help. She seemed okay tonight."

"Yes, she was almost co-operative. It's the end of her year soon – she started all this at the end of one June. I think that's why she's getting twitchy."

"You must like her."

"I do. We all do. She's our Yvonne. It wouldn't be the same without her."

"No, I suppose not." She thought for a moment. "I must say, it's certainly a lovely evening."

"Yes, and there's still quite a bit of daylight left."

"It's such a lovely time of year too."

"Um…" Owen looked like he might have a question in mind.

"Um?"

"Busy?" he asked.

"Not especially."

He smiled.

"Great."

17

By the Water

Following a fifteen-minute walk, Jo and Owen were sitting on a bench by the harbour. The half-mile stretch of open water was so calm, while the boats were bathed in a golden glow. Nearby, a dog splashed playfully in the shallows.

"It's one of my spots," said Owen. "Somewhere to watch the world go by. There's a lot going on if you sit quietly – and I've found the world is happy to ignore you once you reach a certain age."

"I know this place gets busy at the height of summer."

"Yes, crammed full. It's only ours for the next few weeks."

She liked the way he said 'ours' but knew not to read too much into it.

"We'll get it back come September," she said.

Since childhood, she had often wondered about the boats here. Those coming in – where had they been? And those heading out – what adventures lie ahead for them?

"Thanks again for helping with Yvonne," said Owen. "You've only known her a short time."

"She's quite a character. I like her."

A silence settled on them. For Jo, it felt unusually comforting. With Eddie, any silence was filled with concerns about his next move.

"Shall we walk to the next bench?" said Owen. "It's not far."

They set off along a path that led to wilder terrain and views up towards Middle Tolcombe across the water.

"Do you have favourite walks?" Jo asked.

"This is one. Then there's a countryside walk north of town. And I love to go over to Chesil Beach, the heart of the Jurassic Coast. I look for ammonites."

Jo nodded, knowing that ammonites were small fossils distantly related to clams and snails.

"I can't say I've been too lucky," he said. "I have the least impressive collection imaginable."

"I read somewhere you have to go farther west to get really lucky."

"Yes, between Lyme Regis and Charmouth."

"Imagine the time those fossils have been there," said Jo. "Mind you, sometimes I feel I'm not that far behind."

"Really? You feel that old?"

"Well, a bit creaky," she said. "But no, I'm fine. I suppose I'm still trying to work out who I've become recently, because I'm not feeling quite the same person I was."

"That's good – I mean thinking of who you are. I felt the same way when I first retired. Eventually I realised it was still me, just that the circumstances had changed. The best thing, I think, is to avoid suddenly taking on a dozen hobbies or making too many new friends on social media.

You'll never find the real you with all that noise around you."

They found another bench overlooking the water. With the sun a little lower, the shadows were growing longer.

"I used to sit here when I was young," said Owen. "I thought I'd never leave the area."

"But you did."

"My first acting jobs were in touring theatrical productions, and then TV work drew me to London."

"It sounds amazing."

"It was. Then, about three years ago, my dad was ill, so I came to stay for a bit. I was only back a month when he passed away, but something had changed in me and I never left."

Jo thought of her own dad. He never enjoyed a long retirement.

"What about when you were young?" she asked. "You must have got up to a few things."

He laughed a little.

"Yes… being young is a whole different kind of freedom." He thought for a moment before continuing. "I remember being on tour in the Midlands and falling in love for the first time."

"Sounds exciting."

"We were performing 'An Inspector Calls' and I met a girl at a busy café. There was hardly anywhere to sit, so I asked if she'd mind me sharing her two-seater table. We ended up talking for an hour before she had to leave. Amelia…"

"Can you fall in love in an hour?"

"Definitely. But we never had a chance. The next day, the tour moved on to the North-West." He puffed out his cheeks. "Do you know, that was half a century ago."

"It's a lovely memory."

"It destroyed my entire life."

"Really?"

"Well… until I met Suze about a week later."

Jo laughed.

"Happy days."

"Yes… what about you? Any poetic lost loves?"

"Yes." This was insane. She never talked this openly and yet lately she couldn't stop. "I was fifteen… I fell in love with a boy in a day."

"A whole day? I'm jealous. Did he reciprocate your love?"

"Put it this way, I was gazing into his eyes, waiting for him to say, 'Jo, I love you,' but what came out was, 'Jo, I'm moving to Canada.'"

Owen laughed but cut it short. "Sorry, I expect that was quite painful at the time."

"Only for several years."

Time raced by as she went on to tell him about leaving school and moving into the world of work. She also revealed her plan to retire with Martin before his untimely demise.

"That can't have been easy."

"No… so how about you?" she asked. "Did you ever settle down with a partner?"

"Yes, I was married once. 1983 to 1989. Shauna and I were both touring actors. We have a daughter, Holly. She lives in London with her husband, Jacob, and their children."

"So, you're a grandad?"

"Yes, Jack's four, Abigail's two."

"That's brilliant. Do you see them much?"

"Three or four times a year. They come down in the summer. The other times, I get the train up there. I wish I could be a bit more involved, but…"

"London's a long way."

"Yes, although recently I've been thinking about relocating. As I said earlier, I never intended to move back here permanently and it's a big pull in the other direction."

"I'm sure you'll make the right decision."

She hoped it might be a decision to stay, but then berated herself for being selfish.

"I have a son," she said, "but there's currently no sign of a grandchild."

"Never say never."

"Absolutely. Perhaps you should look at properties near your family. At least get an idea of what you could afford in case the time comes."

"It's not that simple. They're talking about moving, so it would be a bit daft if I moved then they moved."

Jo felt sorry for him. But she also felt a tiny bit okay that Owen wouldn't be leaving the south coast just yet.

"Here, I've got some photos," he said, reaching for his phone.

Jack and Abigail were apple-cheeked cherubs.

"They're gorgeous. Do they get up to mischief?"

"One hundred percent."

Jo smiled and gazed out at the view once more. The sun was getting ever lower, glinting on calm waters and the old song, 'Summertime' floated through her mind…

"Come on, time to go," said Owen.

On the way back, they passed a pub. It looked enticing with its hanging baskets full of daises and lobelia, and soft music seeping out through an open window. A chalkboard told of decent pub grub, with the lasagne sounding tempting.

"Perhaps we could go for a meal?" she suggested.

"What, the gang?"

"I thought just us?"

There was a noticeable pause before Owen spoke.
"How does tomorrow evening sound?"
She would have preferred right now, but…
"Tomorrow's fine."

18

Ready, Steady, Go…

With her TV tuned to her regular classical music radio station, Jo was dusting and polishing in the living room. She hadn't planned to, and it didn't need it, but it seemed a reasonable way to spend the first part of Tuesday morning. Into the second week of her new life, she missed chatting with colleagues as she set up meetings, checked over reports, and chased up contracts. Listening to the radio while she squirted *Pledge* and wiped with a soft yellow cloth wasn't the same.

She paused. What else could she do? There had to be a better way to fill the time before her dinner date with Owen.

Then again, maybe there wasn't.

She picked up her mum's photo and squirted the glass. But before she could wipe it clean, a thought began to bubble up – a thought that stretched far into the past and yet felt fresh and invigorating.

Oh Mum… good idea…

She quickly buffed the glass, put the cleaning stuff away, and went out to the local convenience store. Within twenty minutes she was back in the kitchen placing her purchases on the worktop. Butter, eggs, vanilla extract, flour, cocoa powder, and baking powder. Salt and sugar she already had.

"Right, that's everything for brownies."

But something was missing.

A vital ingredient.

She went to the living room. A moment later, she returned with Mum's photo, which she placed on the worktop in an overseer role.

"That's more like it."

It wasn't just that they had worked together making things all those years ago – there had been warmth and encouragement, a sense that great things were possible if you had a mind to follow it through, permission to try and possibly fly…

When she died, so did the encouragement.

"Right, Mum, before we were so rudely interrupted…"

*

Jo bit into the crispy top brownie… and the memories came flooding back. This was the taste.

"Mum, they're perfect. Just like the old days."

Of course, she couldn't recall *exactly* how they had tasted in the old days, but she wasn't going to say that in front of her mum.

As she finished it off, her phone rang. She smiled when she saw the name on the screen.

"Hello, Marilyn."

"Hiya, Jo. Just wanted to let you know we're having a shopping expedition and pub lunch on Friday."

Jo's spirits rose. "That sounds great."

"Good. I'll ping you the details."

"I was also thinking I'd like to do the charity walk."

"Okay, great. I think I sent you the details for that."

"Yes, four miles."

"Four miles of walking very slowly, so think two hours minimum."

Jo couldn't recall the last time she walked for two hours, but it didn't matter. This would be herself joining the Go Club on the town's carnival day to raise money for Sharon's charity.

"Also, you'll need a costume," Marilyn pointed out.

"Yes…"

"Although we might be able to help you with that."

"Okay, great."

"As long as you're sure. We've been training for two months."

"Honestly, I'll be fine. I walked to work for forty years. And getting toys to children in hospital is a great cause."

"Okay, great. We're hoping to raise five hundred pounds, so any help is welcome. We're meeting at Tolcombe Park tomorrow for one of our non-costume practice sessions. I'll ping you the details for that too."

"Great."

After the call, Jo checked the email relating to the charity walk. A week and a half from now, Marilyn would pick everyone up in the minibus – the one her husband used for fishing with his friends – and take them to the back of the beach. From there, in full costume, and as part of the carnival, they would walk four miles collecting money for Sharon's charity.

"Okay, time to test my fitness and work off that brownie."

She found her most comfortable shoes and… headed straight to her laptop where she ordered new training shoes and some jogging attire for express delivery. In the meantime, comfy shoes would have to suffice. She'd simply do an hour. That would be a good test.

Heading south to the seafront, she kept up a steady pace, although this was made easier as it was downhill for half a mile. She did consider it might not be so easy on the way back and, for a mad minute, tried to think of a way that would avoid going uphill. Annoyingly, the laws of physics refused to play ball.

She paused as she reached the front, as she always did. There was something about the sea that required her to stop in awe.

Tourist-wise, the popular end of the beach was reasonably busy, with plenty of people on towels and sun beds, and some playing ball or splashing in the waves. Against a backdrop of glittering water, it looked inviting, but she had work to do.

An almost mile-long walk along the back of the beach felt like a solid effort, with the scene changing from family friendly to dog friendly to just plain rocky and unfriendly. The walk back had her breathing a little harder.

For Jo, a light breeze helped keep her thoughts away from a growing ache in her legs and the temptation to stop for a while. This was a serious business, and she didn't want to come up short.

That said...

Just five minutes!

She found a bench and rested. Nearby, some young people were messing around with an inflatable pink ball. Perhaps they were students taking time out between exams. They seemed to be having fun.

She recalled her own younger days, messing around on the beach – *this* beach. That was how she met Ty. They were both there with friends in search of fun by the sea.

It was strange. Up until recently, she hadn't thought about *amore* for decades. But now, at sixty-eight, she felt a yearning. She supposed it wasn't a genuine yearning; more likely just a reaction to feeling so alone. But even so, it was there.

She rose from the bench and headed for home, surprised by how slowly she walked back. Yes, it was uphill, but having two young schoolgirls ask if she needed help across the road wasn't much of an advert for her all-new 'can-do' outlook.

Back at home, she collapsed onto the sofa.

Two and a half miles. Excellent!

She was pleased to have made a proper start. Hopefully, she would be okay for her practice walk with the Go Club tomorrow. Of course, she had a dinner date with Owen to think about before that…

*

Jo was deep in conversation with Yvonne, telling her how she had been in love with Keith for a whole day, and for a good while after as she weaned herself off him. And then with Ty as they enjoyed a summer of bliss. And yes, she had been married to Martin, and yes, he had been a thoroughly decent man and she wouldn't tolerate anyone suggesting anything other than a happy marriage for which she was grateful. But what of the here and now?

"Owen," said Yvonne. "Isn't the way ahead clear enough? Or do you need a map?"

Jo opened her eyes.

It took a moment to work out where she was. She never fell asleep on the sofa. Absolutely never. Any naps were strictly limited to the bedroom.

She checked the clock.

"Oh… shi…"

In eight minutes, a cab with Owen in the back would pull up outside. She would leap in alongside him and they would head off to Luca's Italian restaurant by the harbour. All she had to do before then was fit in a shower and a change of clothes.

She hauled herself off the sofa.

"Owww…"

While she'd been snoring, someone had poured concrete into her legs. The pain came from her calves mainly, although her lower back was now joining in.

As she groaned her way to the stairs, she imagined herself at the restaurant – all jelly legs and her face collapsed into a pasta.

Upstairs, she undressed and staggered into the shower. The shampoo spent ten seconds in her hair before she washed it out. A few moments later, barely dry, she hurried as best she could to the bedroom.

"Don't rush," she told herself. "You're not desperate."

Pulling on fresh summer trousers, she stumbled to the carpet and groaned.

"Not desperate? Jo Ramsey, you're face down with two feet in one leg."

19

A Little Romance Never Hurt Anyone... Much

Jo and Owen walked into a complete fuss as soon as they entered the restaurant.

"Mr Tate, my friend," gushed Luca, the owner. "So happy to see you again. And your lovely friend. Please, please...."

Jo, her feet and legs aching, barely had time to smile at the barman, waiter, and a dining couple as she and Owen were whisked through to a table on the patio. Here, on timber decking, five of the eight tables were occupied, but theirs was at one end for that added touch of privacy. With a chrome and glass rail separating them from the foreshore, it was perfect for dining while watching the boats come and go across the harbour on a gorgeous summer's evening.

"This is fabulous," she told Luca. "Thank you."

"You're very welcome. It's always nice to see new faces."

He handed them a menu each and placed a wine list on the table.

"Busy, my friend? Any more TV?"

"No, all quiet on that front, Luca."

"They know nothing. Such talent. An Oscar, surely. What is wrong with these people?"

"You're too kind."

"He was in EastEnders," Luca told Jo, loud enough for most of the other patio diners to hear.

She smiled. "So I've heard."

"I was on it twice," Owen explained to Jo. "Both were short-lived characters."

"They know nothing," Luca tutted. "Now, would you like drinks before dinner?"

"Yes, please," said Owen. "Jo?"

She ordered a small gin and tonic with ice and lime, as did Owen. Luca then hurried off, leaving them in peace, although Jo suspected not for long.

"So, you like the table?" Owen enquired.

"It really is lovely." She would have said 'romantic' but didn't want to come across as pushy.

"So, you haven't been here before?"

"No. When I was married, we never went out much beyond golf dinners. And since then, I haven't really…"

The pause hung there for a moment before Owen spoke.

"Well, the food here is great – and you might have noticed the owner is very friendly."

"Yes," said Jo, almost laughing. "I've never had a dinner date with a celebrity before."

"Hardly a celebrity. Now what shall we order?"

Jo ignored the exhaustion in her bones and pored over the menu. It all looked incredibly appetizing.

"I'm not sure. You've been here before. What would you recommend?"

"No, you're the newbie. You choose."

"Um… no, go on. It's your call."

"Okay, well, let's see. How about… the Prawns alla busara and the carbonara?"

"Mmm, that sounds good."

She had never had Prawns alla busara or carbonara before. Martin wouldn't have gone within a million miles of them. It was a good feeling though – just like the week before with Eddie when she'd hurriedly ordered formaggio di capra and ravioli tartufo, and had thoroughly enjoyed them.

"The carbonara's not too harsh on the waistline," said Owen. "They use eggs, which is right. Seriously, some places use cream."

"To be honest I'm only wary of anything in tomato sauce. I worry about getting it over my chin, clothes, tablecloths, walls…"

Owen laughed, which felt terrific and also unusual. She had no track record of making people laugh. All the same, she felt engulfed by warmth and friendship. Owen was lovely.

"There is tomato in the prawns, but really, just tuck a napkin under your chin and don't give it a second thought."

"Okay, I'll try."

"Also…" he mused, still studying the menu, "instead of the carbonara, we could go for the Caprese Chicken. I've had it here before and it's really good. If I recall rightly, it's chicken, melted mozzarella, tomato, and basil pesto."

"Yes, alright. Let's go with that."

She thought momentarily of Eddie. He was Martin's choice and ready to commit long-term, but…

"And wine?"

"Yes, please."

"Any preferences?"

She wasn't used to being consulted on wine choices. On the extremely rare occasions she and Martin had gone out he would order the house white without even a glance in her direction. And although Eddie was a little more adventurous, his consultation skills were hardly extensive.

"Could you choose?" she asked.

"Okay, let's see… I could try to impress you by ordering something obscure, but the house red is always perfect with this kind of food. Unless you'd prefer something else. Honestly, I'd value your opinion."

Again, new phrases. *He would value her opinion.*

"The house red sounds great."

"Right – and the dishes here aren't overloaded so there's always room for an Italian dessert. If you're interested."

"I'd like to see anyone try to stop me."

Again Owen laughed.

She didn't understand it herself. She wasn't trying super-hard to be engaging.

"I think I'm seeing a new side to you, Jo," he said. "You're more relaxed."

Maybe that was it.

"I'm nearly halfway through my second week of retirement. Another fortnight and I'll be like a zen monk."

"Two gin and tonics!" declared Luca, appearing out of nowhere.

This was new too. To be so absorbed in conversation to not notice the world around her. With Martin and Eddie, she noticed every detail.

"And are you ready to order?"

Owen glanced at Jo.

"Are we?"

She nodded. Then she looked up at Luca and tapped the menu.

"Despite all these wonderful choices, we managed to narrow it down."

"Then you must come again and try them all!"

Jo laughed, while Owen eventually managed to convey their order.

Luca approved. Especially the Caprese Chicken.

"Caprese means from Capri, where my mother was born. When she married she moved to Naples, but she taught us to love her birthplace and she always made caprese – caprese salad, caprese chicken, caprese pizza… you understand, yes?"

"Yes," said Jo. "I understand precious memories. My mum also liked to bake and cook…" Perhaps swept up in the moment, something occurred to her. It was silly, but… "And I'd love to learn more. Is Italian food difficult to prepare?"

"No, signora, no. If you enjoy Italian food, you must try. Give it your heart and you will never regret it!"

"It's knowing where to start."

"Start easy. How about cooking something simple but delicious. Pasta alla Norma. This is named for Bellini, the composer of the opera, Norma. It's a wonderful Sicilian dish with melanzana, marinara, and basil."

"Um…?"

"So, melanzana is aubergine to the British and eggplant in America. And marinara is a sauce of tomato, garlic, herbs, and onions, and perhaps a splash of wine."

"It sounds lovely."

"Yes, and if it's not enough for two, don't add more pasta – add a side dish. Something simple like… green beans."

"Oh…"

"You don't like green beans?"

"I love green beans. It's just… well, aren't they a bit plain?"

"What? Green beans, plain?" Luca seemed to take it personally. "Okay, so you roast the beans in the oven, and you add a sprinkle of salt, pepper, and chilli flakes. Another time you can add tahini, or lemon, or Parmesan, or mint, or chives, or onion, or butter, or balsamic vinegar, or toasted sliced almonds. Signora, when you buy a pack of green beans, you have in your hand fifty side dishes!"

Diplomacy was called for.

"Thank you for explaining it, Luca. I'll go with the green beans."

"Excellent!"

Once Luca had departed with their order, and Owen's smirk had died down, she changed the subject.

"So… what's it like, working in television?"

"Oh… television was always good fun, but unless you're in an established role, jobs are often over in a day or two. I did everything I could to get more work and never turned down a role. Well, perhaps once. They asked if I could sing opera. I told them only in the shower."

Jo laughed.

So that's where Delia's shower knowledge came from.

"I love acting," Owen continued. "That's why I was always happiest in a stage role. Becoming a different person for ninety minutes is very liberating. Did you know I've murdered a crooked businessman and made love to a countess all within the space of ten minutes? Not many people can say that."

"No, indeed."

"And don't forget radio. Lots of fond memories there. A live audience of two hundred for a sitcom. An enclosed studio for drama. And half a million people at home, listening. On radio, I've been everywhere from Ancient Rome to the Andromeda galaxy. The Andromeda one was fun. I was a dishonest space station janitor."

"It sounds wonderful."

"It is… was."

Jo considered it. "I've occasionally wished I could be a different character at certain times in my life. Mary Poppins, Hermione Granger, even the Wicked Witch of the West…"

"All characters who can change a situation with a flash of magic?"

"Yes, does that say something about me?"

"Possibly."

Time seemed to speed up as their conversation progressed. Before she knew it, two plates of sizzling Prawns alla busara were brought to their table along with the wine – a Chianti Classico, which Jo's palate was soon appreciating while she studied the label.

"It says it's from Tuscany… mainly the Sangiovese grape."

"Have you ever been to Italy?" Owen asked.

No, when do we leave?

"No, but it's sounds like a fantastic place to visit."

"I've only been a couple of times, but you're right. Tuscany is something special."

He took a sip of wine. She picked up her fork.

"This looks great," she said, trying a prawn. The hint of chilli on her tongue seemed to elevate the tomato and other flavours. "It tastes great too. Do you eat out much?"

"Not really," said Owen. "I'd love to but it's bad for both the waist and the bank balance. But I like to go wild occasionally."

"Wild? At our age?"

"Especially at our age!"

Jo tried to imagine it, but Owen interrupted.

"We *are* talking about food?"

"Of course, Owen. Whatever else would we talking about?"

She was surprising herself. It was as if both he and she were getting a glimpse of a hidden Jo. She felt more alive right now than she had in years.

Owen took another sip of his wine while she speared another prawn.

"So why did you retire?" she asked. "I thought actors could go on and on."

Owen considered it.

"We can go on and on, as you say – but only if we continue to network like crazy. When your best work is a long way back in an ever-receding past, it can be better to call it a day. I know actors in their seventies who proudly declare they're still working, despite going one, two, three years between paid jobs."

"Really?"

"Outsiders sometimes wonder why the industry is full of people constantly praising their peers…"

"You mean luvvies?"

"Not a term I like, but yes. Everyone going around saying how wonderful everyone else is. It's a survival mechanism. The pond is actually much smaller than you might think and you're always working with someone you've met before."

"So describing another actor as average might lead to disaster."

"Another actor, producer, director… but look, how about we learn a little more about you, Jo. I really don't know much."

"Oh… well… I've never done anything as exciting as acting. As I told you yesterday, admin is busy but it's hardly memorable. I can't look back at a day ten years ago when I put a great schedule together. The company has interesting clients though. We did the marketing for a Shakespeare festival recently. My role wasn't creative, but it was interesting to be so close to it all."

"Yes, but what about *you*, Jo? What about away from work? Say, over the past twenty years?"

Jo tried to think.

"Well, twenty years ago… my son would have already left home, so no running around after him. Martin, yes, he was a golf nut, so we didn't do much together. We tended to follow our own interests."

"So, outside of work, let's say over the past ten years, how have you spent your own personal free time?"

"Um… after work, I'm happy to… I mean I *was* happy to make a simple dinner and watch TV. Once you add in shopping for groceries and doing the washing…"

Owen put his glass down.

"Jo, how can I help you with retirement? Shall we go through your ideas?"

Suddenly, this no longer felt like a date. And it certainly wasn't the open-ended fun of earlier. It occurred to her that while Owen was a lovely guy, he wasn't going to be her retirement partner. That was fine though.

"Are you adventurous?" Owen asked.

There was the truth of it.

"Not really," she said as the relaxed Jo vanished.

A few weeks ago, she feared retirement would be a period of her life she would spend alone. It seemed she'd been right.

Of course, she could change all that. All she had to do was wait until tomorrow lunchtime and then say, "Eddie, it's all systems go."

20

Part of the Club

Jo hummed a vague tune while she buttered the toast. She hadn't done that in a long time. It wasn't so much a sign of contentment midway through her second week of retirement, but more her determination to at least look contented.

In truth, she wanted everything to be different.

On the radio, Pippa from East Yorkshire had just emailed a dedication to the morning show for her daft, darling hubby Harry who never forgot birthdays or anniversaries and always made her feel special. So now the DJ was playing 'I Will Always Love You.'

Impervious to Whitney's warbling, Jo hummed her vague tune louder as her teeth crunched down on the toast.

Of course, the hurt wasn't purely emotional. Her feet and legs still ached from all the walking. On reflection, she probably could have done without the impending meet-up with the club in an hour, but a promise was a promise. And if Jo had one consistent trait in her DNA, it was a dislike of letting people down.

She glanced at the photo on the end of the worktop.

"Shall we do something together, Mum?"

It didn't take them long to decide on what – especially as Jo had all the ingredients in for a cookie recipe on her phone.

"Okay... softened butter, light brown muscovado sugar, granulated white sugar, vanilla extract, a large egg, plain flour, bicarbonate of soda, salt, chocolate chips... yep..."

She fired up the oven and lined a couple of baking sheets with non-stick paper.

Her phone pinged. It was an email from Ollie. They had worked something out she might be interested in.

She stared at the screen. This was good, wasn't it?

Wondering what she actually wanted from life, she placed the softened butter and sugar into a bowl and beat them into a creamy mix. Next she beat in the vanilla extract and the egg. Then she sifted the flour, bicarbonate of soda and salt into the bowl and mixed everything together with a wooden spoon.

Finally, she added the chocolate chips.

The doorbell rang. It was a delivery of sporty red jogging attire and purple training shoes. She felt fitter already.

Back in the kitchen, she spooned thirty small measures onto the trays, and baked them for ten minutes. By then, they were light brown around the edges and just a little soft in the middle.

After that, it was just a matter of leaving them on the tray for a short while before transferring them to a cooling rack.

*

Jo's sporty attire might have look all-action, but its impact was minimal. In truth, she felt every one of her sixty-eight years. Even the three-minute walk to Marilyn's took six – although it felt more like twenty. Hopefully, the practice walk in the park wouldn't be more than thirty or forty minutes. Any longer and she might seize up.

Marilyn and her husband Gavin lived in a neat, yellow brick, end of terrace Victorian house with a dark crimson front door and polished brass knocker.

As Jo rang the bell, the door flew open.

"I spotted you through the window," Marilyn declared with enough enthusiasm for both of them.

"Great, so Tolcombe Park, here we come."

"Actually, the next stop is Ruth's."

"Oh, doesn't she live beyond the park?"

"It'll only add another twenty minutes."

Jo hoped her groan wasn't audible.

"What about Yvonne?" she asked as they set off down the street.

"She's meeting us for the final half hour. She said she didn't feel up to a full session."

"Oh right."

Sensible girl!

Jo hoped the aches would ease off once she was fully loosened up. The charity walk in support of Sharon's chosen cause was important. She wanted to be ready for it.

"Oh, and good news. Sharon has a costume you can use. A Knight of the Round Table. If that's okay?"

"Great. So… what about Owen? Is he practising today?"

"He's busy, but he's pretty fit. Frankly, I reckon he could keep going for hours."

Jo pondered that for a millisecond before telling herself to stop being so juvenile.

*

It felt strange-but-good to be walking in the park with Ruth and Marilyn – especially on the other side of the pond to the bench where Jo had stopped for lunch that time. There was an elderly man sitting there now, looking across the water. At least he couldn't condemn them for messing around in daft costumes. All he would see were sweaty fellow oldsters walking five times around the park at a reasonable pace for no apparent reason.

Jo didn't mind though. She was with her new friends. And perhaps this was the life for her going forward.

Unless she went back to work.

It wasn't lost on her that Jennifer and her hubby were only a bus ride away and, with Jen now staying on, it was likely they wouldn't mind her tagging along for the morning commute. As for the evenings, she could return home by bus and leave them in peace. Arriving home an hour later than usual wouldn't be an issue.

"How do you feel being part of the club?" said Marilyn.

They were all a little out of breath by now.

"Great, thanks," Jo puffed.

"Have you thought of becoming a full member?"

"Oh, I didn't realise…"

"It's not compulsory," said Ruth. "And everyone's a full member really. It's just something Melanie came up with. A bit of fun. She's the one I started the club with. We were best friends."

"She passed away last year," said Marilyn.

Jo could almost feel Ruth's loss.

"Then I'd like to become a full member. Whatever it takes. As long as it doesn't involve wearing a snorkel or jumping out of a plane."

"You'll be fine," said Ruth. "To become a full member, you must do something crazy for yourself, something worthwhile for charity, and something wonderful for the community."

"In the first twelve months," said Marilyn.

"No pressure," said Ruth, "and we'll help with ideas. And really, you don't have to do it."

Jo considered it for a moment.

"I'd like to."

"Great," said Marilyn.

"Take some time to think up what you'd like to do," said Ruth.

Marilyn nodded. "Last year, Mandy and Mitch renewed their wedding vows on top of the Millennium Dome, did a round-the-park juggling marathon for a heart charity, and arranged an outdoor treasure hunt for their grandson's class at school."

"Wow, brilliant," said Jo. "They certainly set the bar high."

In some ways, she still felt as if she were acting at being a Go Club member, rather than naturally fitting in. But from now on, that would change.

"So," said Marilyn. "Do you feel you're beginning to get to grips with retirement?"

"I'm trying my best."

"When I retired, I took up piano lessons, an online history degree, and gardening. Within a few weeks, I knew I'd just filled my days with things to do rather than find out what the real me needed. Ruth helped me see there was no rush. I didn't need to work everything out in one go."

"I'm beginning to think we're not so different," Jo admitted.

"It takes time to find the right things," said Ruth.

Marilyn concurred. "My enjoyment in life is seeing friends a couple of times a week and doing whatever takes my fancy in between. Gardening? Yes, if I want. A history degree? No, but I do enjoy reading the occasional book and watching documentaries on TV. Piano lessons? Seriously, Jo, I've got ten thumbs. In the end, it's up to each of us to create the kind of life we want to live."

"And who we want to live it with?"

"That too. Very much so."

They walked on a for a bit, passing by the old bandstand. Back in the mid-1960s, Jo used to sit there with her gran listening to a brass band when all her friends were raving about the Beatles and the Stones.

"Are you seeing any of your old work friends?" Marilyn asked.

"I'm not sure yet."

And that was the truth.

She wondered. Should she just copy Marilyn – seeing friends a couple of times a week and doing whatever took her fancy in between. Could it really be that simple to create the kind of life she wanted to live?

21

Use Your Imagination

Lunch with Eddie was a ham sandwich at her dining table. Nothing wrong with that, especially as she wanted to be friendly without making him feel special.

"I hate to see you in pain," he said.

She hadn't intended to tell him how much she ached from her Go Club session at the park, but it didn't take a doctor to spot her discomfort.

"I'm okay."

"It's your own fault for walking so far."

"It's for a good cause."

She tried stretching her lower back with a slow snaking motion.

"Wouldn't it be easier to give them money?"

"That's not the point."

"I thought that was exactly the point. It's for charity, right?"

"Yes, but it's the joining in that's important."

"Why?"

"Because…"

"Jo, you're in agony."

"No, I'm not," she insisted, although as lies went, it wasn't a very convincing one. Even her aches had aches.

"Well, it's your life."

"It's fun, Eddie."

"Fun?"

"You know what I mean."

"Hmm… well… nice ham, by the way."

"You're welcome."

Being with Eddie… would that really solve her retirement worries? The two of them watching TV together? Her doing his washing and cooking…?

"And nice bread," he added.

"I'm glad you like it."

Would life with Eddie be better than life alone?

Possibly.

And perhaps their bedtime encounters would only be once or twice a year – and she could pretend he was Owen.

She gasped and shut the thought down. It was outrageous, and possibly illegal. She could only imagine what her gran would have made of it.

Of course, there was the other possibility – the idea of going back to Bonner's. Then she would have her equilibrium restored by having workplace colleagues and a purpose in life. Under those circumstances, she wouldn't need anyone else.

Eddie snapped his fingers, as if he'd had a eureka moment.

"How about getting an encore job?"

She hadn't told him about Bonner's and didn't plan to, but she was surprised he was now attempting to push her back out to work.

"What kind of encore job?"

"Come on, Jo, use your imagination."

"That's not very helpful."

"There's a woman near me who delivers small parcels. Or you could work in a library."

"It's not just the work, Eddie."

"Then what?"

"I miss being valued, having a purpose, a structure."

"The woman who delivers the parcels has all that."

"I miss the people at Bonner's. I came to know them over a long period of time. I'm not someone who seeks out a situation where I'd be doing work I've never done before with people I don't know."

"Look, an encore job is low pressure. You'd have fun and get paid."

"So why haven't you taken one?"

"What? No, look, I'm happy being retired. It's never been a problem for me. You're the one who needs that kind of interaction. I'd be happy to stay here on my own while you're out. Honestly, it doesn't bother me in the slightest."

"You've worked it all out in a very logical way."

"I'm glad you think so."

"There's another option though. Volunteering."

Eddie nodded. "Yes, you could volunteer for something."

"I meant you!"

"Me?"

"Yes, you – you could volunteer for something."

"Why would I want to volunteer for something? I've already told you, I'm happy here with you."

Jo didn't like it. He was talking as if him moving in had been agreed. But if she threw him out, where would that leave her? And could she even do it? She had never ditched anyone before. Not ever. It felt like a betrayal, and possibly bordered on cruelty. How did people get rid of other people?

After lunch, Eddie started making exaggerated stretching actions.

"I think a little rest and relaxation is in order. What do you say?"

She wasn't sure what to say.

"Come on," he said.

He led her into the hall and up the stairs. She followed physically, but her mind was racing.

Is this what you want?

At her bedroom door, he entered, but she halted on the threshold.

"Nice room," he said.

He plonked himself down on the edge of the bed and patted the space beside him.

"I once had a long chat with Martin about our wives," he said. "This was back when I was with Dawn. I told him how I envied him."

"Oh?" She'd met Dawn a couple of times at golf dinners. She'd seemed nice.

"Dawn and I were together, but it was already over, if you know what I mean. Whereas Martin said he was with the most loyal person there was. That's you, Jo."

It was only when he patted the space beside him again that she realised she had yet to enter the room.

But would a relationship with Eddie be so bad?

"Let's get into bed," he said softly.

Still on the threshold, she wondered. Would this be thirty seconds? Or was he on those pills and she'd be there till Sunday?

The moment drew closer. She could feel it in the air – an intensity of expectation.

Loyal Jo. Her next move would define the rest of her life.

"I have a request," she said in a small but steadfast voice.

"I'm game. What did you have in mind?"

"I'd like you to leave."

"What?"

"I don't see us having a future."

"But what about Martin's take on all this. On us?"

"In case you hadn't noticed, Martin isn't here. And I'd prefer it if you would stop mentioning his name."

"You're probably nervous. It's perfectly understandable."

"It's time to go, Eddie."

"Yes, but… I mean… well… I've already taken the pill."

"What?"

"It says on the pack wait thirty minutes."

"Please go home."

"Are you sure?"

"Yes, I'm sure."

"And what am I supposed to do with…?"

In her mind she said, "Use your imagination." Out loud she simply said, "Sorry," and led him down to the front door.

*

Jo was enjoying an Italian cookery show she had recorded. The chef was commending the merits of the delicious home cooking and baking his mother used to do. It made her think of Luca's mother, which in turn made her think of her own mum.

What goodies they made. Crispy top brownies, bread pudding, apple pie, blueberry muffins, lemon drizzle cake, cheese and shallot flan, chicken and mushroom puff pie, steak and ale pie, beef suet pudding…

"It's really simple," the chef was saying. "We have some bread, so we'll cut it into slices and make bruschetta. All we need is tomatoes, basil, olive oil, and black pepper. I know you'll be very happy eating this."

Cooking didn't feel like a hobby. It felt like something more. Maybe it really was a way forward.

So…?

For dinner, there were fishfingers in the freezer, which would have suited her gran, and Martin too. Mum had been different. She never cooked Italian, but so what? Mum had always been the one to try new things.

So, try something different.

Bruschetta?

No, bigger and bolder.

But what?

She googled some options.

Luca's recommendation, pasta alla Norma, looked good, but so did the stuffed pasta shells, and the Tuscan seafood stew.

In the end she settled for something Owen had suggested in the restaurant before they switched to Caprese Chicken.

"Mum, I'm going to make the carbonara. Wish me luck."

*

Jo studied her list and checked it against the items in her basket. She had the garlic cloves, flat leaf parsley, chives, and unsalted butter. And now, in the cheese aisle, she had the pecorino and parmesan. But she couldn't locate the pancetta…

In the end, she asked a member of staff for help.

"Try the bacon section."

Jo's eyes widened.

"Pancetta is bacon?"

Who knew?

It didn't matter. She was buying the ingredients for a carbonara, and it was fun.

On the way to find the pancetta, she studied the rest of the list. Eggs, spaghetti, sea salt, and black peppercorns.

"And not forgetting…"

She jotted an additional item at the bottom of the list.

'Italian white wine.'

*

Jo poured herself a glass of Soave. She was ready to cook for one. Of course, the recipe on her phone was for four, but it was a simple enough equation. First, she put the pasta on to boil. Then…

"Here we go, Mum. Peel and chop the garlic…"

As she did so, she enjoyed getting to know the texture and the sharp, pungent aroma.

Next, she cut off a shard of cheese for a research-based nibble.

"Mmm, that is seriously good."

Eating a second piece, she read the overview of the recipe again.

The idea was to gently fry the garlic and pancetta in the butter. At the same time, she would cook and drain the spaghetti. And also at the same time, she would wash and chop the parsley and chives, while shaving the cheese, and whisking the egg in a bowl. And then, finally, in a flash of magic, she would stir everything into the drained but still hot pasta – its heat effectively cooking the egg without turning it into an omelette.

"Right, all we need are five hands."

She opted to get the egg sorted early as that might get messy under pressure.

"So, one medium egg."

She took one from the carton and eyed it suspiciously.

"Hmm, these look small."

A decision was required.

"Two medium eggs."

After that, things went downhill. Perhaps the pasta, when cooked and drained, didn't stay hot for long enough. And maybe there was too much egg? Whatever the reason, it didn't look appetising.

Or edible.

"Oh well, more wine."

But something was different. A disaster yes, but it hadn't put her off. If anything, she wanted to try again. Obviously, not right away though.

As a makeshift compromise, she carefully removed all the spaghetti to leave the rest of the cooked ingredients covered in gooey egg. She then added another egg and a splash of milk and turned up the heat.

"One omelette coming up!"

22

Men, Ha!

A boat chugged into the harbour from the sea, its plain indigo hull enhanced by dayglo orange ropes, a red and white lifebuoy, and an imperious herring gull perched on the cabin roof. With the sun rising high in a pale azure sky, it was undoubtedly going to be another scorcher. Hence the t-shirts and shorts Jo and Marilyn were wearing as they waited for Ruth and Yvonne by the ferry point on the South Tolcombe quayside.

The ferry wasn't the most efficient way for them all to get to Middle Tolcombe. While it was a reasonable choice for Jo and Marilyn, it wasn't so direct for Ruth, who lived three-quarters of the way to the Middle Tolcombe quay, or Yvonne, who would be picked up by Ruth's cab on route. But on such mornings as these, for those free of commitments, a boat trip across beautiful, calm, inland waters offered nothing less than the wow factor.

"Ah, that Friday feeling," said Marilyn.

She sucked in a lungful of fresh sea air and exhaled noisily.

Jo smiled. Yes, that Friday feeling – the one a retired person could enjoy any day of the week.

"The end of week two," she mused.

"I wouldn't count the weeks," Marilyn advised. "When we retire, it's forever."

"Yes, although…"

But Marilyn was suddenly waving. Ruth and Yvonne were coming along.

"What a lovely day," said Ruth as the two duos merged and swapped hellos.

"All ready to board the boat?" Marilyn asked.

"Dang, I forgot my pirate outfit," said Yvonne.

It was only a short wait for the ferry, and they were soon aboard. After all the tiring walking of the past couple of days, it was a wonderful feeling to sit down and glide gracefully across the water. A sense of adventure arose in Jo's chest. A sense of opportunity and possibilities…

"This is the life," Ruth extolled.

"Absolutely," said Jo.

As they moved farther up the harbour, she searched for where she and Owen had sat. But everything looked so different from the water. That was okay though – she would find it on her map app another time.

"Hello and ahoy!" Yvonne called to someone on a passing vessel. It made Jo laugh. Had her new friend ever worried about what other people might think? Probably not – and good for her!

Soon, their voyage took them from open water into the wide mouth of the river that would deliver them into the town. That's when Jo's phone pinged. It was an email from Terry.

He was offering her a twelve-month freelance contract starting on the thirtieth of the month. The first few days at Avalon House and then at Skyline. He explained that they were taking on five new staff and that he needed people who knew the ropes, who he could rely on, who he could trust.

Right…

So, he didn't trust Nina or Kim, meaning she could be back at work ten days from now and forget retirement for a whole year. For a while, it sucked the life out of the boat trip.

At Middle Tolcombe's quayside, they disembarked and stretched their legs. Everything felt so leisurely, as if they had all the time in the world. And perhaps that was their gift in retirement – to have all the time in the world for as long as it lasted.

First, a stroll past the old priory had them stopping in its glorious grounds and taking photos, including a fantastic group selfie of smiling, happy faces. Then, not long after, they were at the start of the old High Street with its Georgian era shops.

"Ah! That lamp!" said Yvonne peering into a window.

To Jo, it looked a little exotic with its fiery red base and yellow shade with jagged edges.

Yvonne nudged her.

"What do you think?"

Jo wasn't sure.

"It's not the usual thing you see in people's homes."

"My thoughts exactly!" said Yvonne, going in.

They wandered into and out of more shops, just browsing and enjoying the day. Jo even managed to shake off her long-departed grandmother's view that idle hands did the Devil's work, because it was such a pleasure to be hanging out like a carefree teenager on a summer break.

At one point though, she noticed something odd with Marilyn – as if a dark cloud had flashed across her face. She seemed to be looking across the street to where a man, possibly in his sixties, had just emerged from a café.

An hour or so later, it was lunchtime, which meant a short stroll to The Queen's Head, a lovely, old-fashioned pub with oak beams, comfy seats, and gentle chatter. Jo could imagine, come winter, the huge stone fireplace being lit to provide a warming glow. Now though, in sunny June, it was more a case of getting an ice-cold drink and trying to catch the breeze from a small electric fan behind the bar.

It was as Jo was taking her first sip of chilled non-alcoholic lager that Owen appeared in the doorway. He looked relaxed in a golden sand summer jacket, light blue open-necked shirt, and blue jeans. Admittedly, some things never went out of style.

As he approached, Jo tried to smile in a neutral way, as she might when greeting a delivery driver.

"Hi all," he said as he joined three of the four of them – Marilyn being absent.

They returned the greeting, while Ruth ordered him a small cider.

"You missed the shopping expedition," said Jo, noting that he smelled good too, fresh from a shower with a hint of something cedar.

"Too right," he joked. "Hands up those who've spent all their money."

"Hey," Yvonne protested, "forty-five pounds for a lamp is a bargain!"

Jo raised her eyes at the thought of the item to be delivered to Yvonne's place tomorrow.

"Hello Owen," said Marilyn, returning from the other side of the pub. "Good news, everyone, I've set up a darts match."

"Bring it on!" roared Yvonne.

Before Jo could say a word, Marilyn was handing her a set of darts and leading them over to the board.

"I can't play darts," she protested. "I'd be a danger to the public."

"Take a few practice throws," Marilyn insisted.

Jo felt the weight of three darts in her hand.

"Okay then."

She threw them, one after the other, hitting treble 17, the rim of the board, and a picture of a fishing boat.

"Abandon ship," gasped Yvonne.

"Perhaps you could keep score?" Marilyn suggested, handing Jo a stick of chalk, and pointing to the scoreboard.

During the game, Yvonne asked Jo how things were progressing with Eddie.

"I'm no longer with him," she said.

It felt good to get it off her chest among friends. She really was free now. Owen failed to react though, which was fine.

A little later, following several rounds of throws from which Ruth emerged victorious, their lunch order of sandwiches and side salads was ready. Jo even went for a garlic dressing and didn't worry a jot about what Martin used to call hostile breath.

To enhance their enjoyment of lunch, they opted to sit outside in the potted plant sanctuary of the beer garden under a table with a big blue and white striped umbrella.

"Cheers all," said Yvonne, raising a glass of white wine. "And yes, I know I said I'd quit drinking on weekdays, but it's Friday. Seriously, you don't need to stand on tiptoes to see the weekend."

"Hooray for the weekend," said Jo, happy to join in.

"Is that right the fishing season's over?" Yvonne asked Marilyn.

"Only for rivers. My Gavin would fish in a puddle if he could, but they go to a lake where you don't need a license."

Jo was sympathetic.

"Have you ever thought of going with him?" she asked.

Marilyn's eyes widened.

"No," she said, clearly using a small answer to mask a bigger one.

"Oh well," said Jo, sympathetically.

After lunch, while Owen popped inside to chat with an elderly chap he knew, four young men took over the next table. Jo had to smile. She recalled sitting with girl friends in a pub beer garden just like this one half a century ago when a group of young men came to sit at the next table. Of course, back then, there were the hundred glances the girls received, and the inevitable chatting up… and the boys lifting their table to be nearer.

Marilyn stood up. "I'm just going to stretch my legs."

Jo watched her wander off to the edge of the beer garden, where it bordered a bubbling stream. She gave it a moment and then went to join her.

"What a glorious day, Marilyn."

"Yes, it is."

"I know it's none of my business, but I hope everything's alright."

"Everything's fine, Jo."

"Well, that's good. It's a lovely way to spend the day, isn't it. Browsing in shops, a pub lunch…"

"The problem with Gavin is he's married to his friends. Fishing days, cricket days, football nights, pub nights…"

"Right."

"I'm tired of just being there to tidy up behind him, to put food on the table… I'm just tired."

"The thing with you, Marilyn, is you're a good person. Reliable. Trustworthy."

Marilyn looked away.

"That's not strictly true."

"Oh?"

"I had an affair a few years back. Gavin doesn't know, but I do."

Jo felt uncomfortable – and it wasn't just the hot sun beating down. She didn't wish to hear about private matters.

But something struck her, and it struck hard.

If she and Marilyn were friends – actual, real friends – then her own sensibilities had no place here. No universal power had declared Jo good and Marilyn bad. They were just two ordinary people trying to make sense of their later years. If such friendships could be rocked or even destroyed by such a revelation, then surely the whole thing was a sham.

"Yes, so…" This was hard for Jo, but she galvanised herself. "Would you like to talk about it?"

"Thanks, but it was a moment of weakness. I just craved love. But I won't pursue it again. Out of respect."

"For Gavin?"

"For myself."

Marilyn stared into the water.

"Life…" said Jo, trying to be philosophical but without the words to follow it up.

"Exactly."

Jo joined her in staring into the water.

"The man I had the affair with…" said Marilyn. "I saw him earlier."

Thought so.

"Do you often see him out and about?"

"No, he lives in Bournemouth, so…"

"A chance encounter."

"Yes. I don't miss him or anything. It's just occasionally I remember how he made me feel."

"What's his name and address?" Jo joked. She immediately withdrew it. "Sorry."

"Don't be. But don't forget, the guilt scooped out my innards."

"Yes, of course. So, is there a way forward with Gavin?"

"He doesn't see a problem."

"Have you ever told him how you feel?"

"No. Do you think I should?"

"I don't know. It just seems… well, you shouldn't have to go on like this."

"Amen to that."

Again, they stared into the water – this time until Jo spoke.

"I'm sure you'll find a way to move forward."

Marilyn gave a thin smile.

"That's what scares me."

Returning to the table, Jo realised how much she cared about her new friends. Ruth looking serious… Yvonne being jolly about something…

"…no, next week, but it's strictly just Owen and Miranda."

"Fair enough," said Ruth.

Jo stepped away to check her phone for… anything. It was a few minutes before she re-joined them, by which time they were rising from the table.

"Nice lunch," said Ruth.

"Mmm, could've done with a dessert," said Yvonne.

"We had a dessert. Fruit salad."

"As far I'm concerned, dessert hasn't been consumed unless there's chocolate and cream coming out of my ears. Still, on the plus side, zero calorie fruit salad means less weight to carry during my afternoon of passion with the bloke from the library."

Jo stared at her.

Yvonne grinned. "Joke. Not happening." Her smile fell away to leave a more earnest expression. "Were you serious the other day – about liking classical music?"

"Yes, of course. You've probably worked out I'm not much of a joker."

"Only there's a Chopin piano recital in Bournemouth next month. I could get a couple of tickets."

Jo felt a warm glow.

"Yes, I'd love to come. Thanks."

"Leave it with me," said Yvonne with a wink. "I've heard there's a man who knows a woman whose brother works with someone who might, possibly know someone. Either that or I'll just try the official website."

"I'll leave it in your capable hands, Yvonne."

Just then, she spotted Owen exiting the pub's side door and heading for their table. She missed having him as a potential partner, but she had ditched Eddie regardless of other factors. Luckily, she was mature enough emotionally to have Owen in her life as a friend.

So, as a friend, she asked him about his allotment.

"I'm heading over there soonish. Fancy coming along?"

Jo's spirits lifted considerably, although she tried to play it cool – despite Yvonne's elbow not-so-secretly prodding her ribs.

"I'd love to."

She wouldn't allow herself thoughts of how it might turn out though. He was taking her to a veggie patch not Venice.

23

A Small Plot of Land

In glorious afternoon sunshine, Jo and Owen made their way beyond the High Street and up to the town's main through road. Here, the traffic was busier, but when they crossed, they were soon heading up a quiet side street.

In all, it was a twenty-minute walk from the pub and Jo was beginning to see how he kept in shape. He was hardly ever off his feet. Her own feet, however, felt like two iron weights hanging from legs made of thin elastic.

"Do you walk everywhere?" she asked.

"Almost," he said. "I do have a car, but yes, I try to walk as much as possible."

At the end of the street, a lane ran off to the right. Here, houses lined one side, while the allotment grounds sat on the other. Beyond the allotments was beautiful open countryside.

"Just up here," said Owen.

Through the animal-proof mesh fencing, Jo could already see five or six busy enthusiasts scattered about. In the far corner, a lazy plume of smoke suggested one of them had a small incinerator on the go.

They entered through a set of tall gates and strolled along a straight path that cut right across the site. Some of the plots were stunning, with robust plants, flowers, and early fruits. Others featured a greater degree of younger, budding plants with the promise of plenty to come during late summer.

Near the end of the path, they turned right up a narrow track.

"I'm just up on the left."

Owen's patch was the size of a tennis court and had been divided into various production zones. Some of these were in full swing; others had barely got started. In the far corner sat a small shed, a compost bin, and a rusty wheelbarrow. A little patch of paradise? For Owen, it clearly was.

"You're in luck," he said, "I have two folding chairs."

Jo would have jumped for joy but lacked the energy.

Producing a key, Owen removed the shed's padlock and opened the door. Half-stepping inside, he retrieved the chairs, which he leaned against the side of shed. He then grabbed two wide-brimmed straw hats from a shelf, placing one on his head and handing one to Jo.

A few moments later, they were taking the weight off their feet. It was so peaceful, with just the chirping of small birds and the distant sound of a barely active wind chime.

"This is lovely," said Jo.

"You're not alone in thinking that. There's a ten-year waiting list for a plot."

"Wow, so no point in deciding to take it up when we retire then."

"Not unless you apply for one ten years beforehand."

"So, how did you get one?"

"It was my dad's. I used to come and help him when I had the time – and as a working actor, I often had more time not working than I'd like to admit. Anyway, I didn't know it then, but I was effectively networking. When Dad passed away, the committee approached me."

Jo took it in, the sights, the smells. The air was so still she could hear bees from twenty feet away.

"The grandchildren have been here a couple of times."

"Jack and Abigail? That's great."

"Yes, I've had them hard at it, digging and what have you."

"I bet they have fun."

"Not as much fun as on the beach, but yes. Kids like getting muddy. Parents, not so much."

Jo could imagine the extra laundry.

"So, what do you grow?" she asked.

"All sorts. Right now, I've got new potatoes, peas, asparagus, spring onions, chillies, peppers, lettuce, watercress, blackcurrants, strawberries, and raspberries."

"You could supply supermarkets."

"Hardly – but it's nice having a range I can enjoy and share. Soon, we'll have courgettes, cucumbers, broccoli, tomatoes… then it'll be potatoes, leeks, onions… and, into winter, carrots, cabbage, and parsnips. I might have left one or two things out."

This wasn't her passion, but she could see how it was his. And that made things clearer. Anyone could start something, but it took effort to keep it going.

"I don't have an established passion like yours," she said, "but I think I might have one starting."

"Sounds interesting. What is this hidden passion that's about to leap out and surprise everyone?"

"Cooking and baking," she announced confidently. "Although I'd like to concentrate more on cooking. In fact, Italian cooking. That's not too ambitious, is it?"

"No, it's a good call. I like it."

"Confession time. I tried and failed recently. Pasta carbonara? More like pasta disaster. The thing is though… something's different. I wasn't put off. I wanted to try again and get better at it."

"That's great. And if it's fresh organic fruit and veg you need, just let me know. Most stuff I can let you have at very low cost; some I can let you have for free."

Jo felt a warm glow, which seemed to be happening more and more since she hooked up with the Go Club.

"Thanks. Having fresh ingredients to hand makes me even more determined to get going with this. I'll need plenty of practice before I inflict it on the Go Club though."

"I'm sure we'll all be willing guinea pigs. Apart from carbonara, what other recipes are you thinking of?"

"I'm not a hundred percent sure yet. Right now, I'm just curious about how chefs use herbs and spices, and how they match ingredients. Take chilli – not to blow people's heads off, but to enhance, to bring out the other flavours, to give the tongue a little zing…"

"Hey, this does sound like the start of a passion. Just let us all know when to be there."

An idea popped into her head.

"I might mock up a menu for fun. The kind of things I'd like to cook."

"I like it."

"Obviously, the wine list wouldn't be so extensive."

"Only until we all turn up with enough to float a boat."

"Thanks Owen. For the encouragement."

"You're welcome."

She wondered – this might not be Venice, but could it be the start of something that might lead there? After all, wasn't she kidding herself about friendship being enough?

"You might have heard in the pub, but I'm not with Eddie. We've split up."

"Yes, I heard."

Owen didn't leap straight in. Perhaps he was too wise for that. Or too stubborn.

He got up.

"I just need to check the tomatoes."

While he went off to remove a few rogue side shoots with his secateurs, she wondered if to volunteer more information. Did 'friend' Owen need to know all the details?

"With Eddie… well… let's just say it was going to work really well for him, but not for me."

"I don't know if I'm ready for a relationship," he said, examining a plant.

"Oh."

"I'm not young anymore and I'm used to being on my own."

"Yes, of course. Me too."

She felt awkward. Eddie had never been someone she could love, but Owen was different. That said, having neither was better than settling for the wrong man. At least she'd managed to get that right.

"I'm just going to pick some strawberries," he said. "Won't be a tick."

She watched him go off to the other side of the plot. Perhaps she'd retired at the wrong time in the wrong place. Then again, Terry was offering her a role starting on the thirtieth. She could forget retirement for twelve months.

A sense of loyalty built on a forty-year association with Bonner's bubbled up. They needed her and it didn't feel right letting them down. It would be good for her wellbeing too. She would be back in a world she understood thanks to decades of full-time engagement. Her couple of weeks of retirement felt lightweight by comparison.

With any lingering misgivings set aside, she pulled out her phone and emailed Terry to say she would be very happy to come back.

Yes, work would give her a purpose once more. It would end the uncertainty around being alone and feeling empty.

And the fun part? She had ten days to say farewell to her new friends.

"Right, we have the strawberries," said Owen. "It's time you met Sharon."

24

Sharon

During a leisurely twenty-minute walk that took them halfway back to the Parkside district, Owen told Jo a little more about Sharon and her efforts during the club's early days. He also told her about Sharon's health situation, which wasn't good.

Walking in through St Mary's open wrought iron gates, Jo beheld a lovely old Victorian building set in manicured grounds. It looked so inviting. Except this was a hospice and Jo didn't much like the idea of visiting a stranger here. She felt the patients would probably prefer to be left in peace.

Inside, with high ceilings and large open windows, the heat of the day dropped away. The feeling of being an intruder though... that intensified as their heels click-clacked along an otherwise silent corridor.

Sitting up in an adjustable bed, Sharon's thin hair and skinny forearms made her look older than her early seventies. However, despite seeming weary, she brightened on seeing Owen.

"Hey!" she exclaimed, although her voice lacked strength.

"Hello, Sharon. How are you?"

"I'm okay. Who have you brought with you?"

"This is Jo, the new member I mentioned."

"Ah, I've been hearing all about you, Jo. It's lovely to meet you in person."

"That's very kind. And thank you for the loan of the knight's costume."

"You're very welcome."

Still feeling a little uncertain, Jo took in the bright and airy room with its large window overlooking the grounds to the rear of the building. The overall effect was of a calm, tranquil space.

"I brought these," said Owen, placing the strawberries in a small glass bowl on the window ledge. She would probably only eat one or two, or maybe none, but that didn't seem to be the point. For Jo, it felt intense. Everyone knew the situation.

Sharon meanwhile smoothed down an imaginary crinkle in the bed covers.

"Our little club… I'm very grateful to everyone."

"Me too," said Owen.

"Yvonne was in yesterday reading the news and chatting."

"She does that with Delia too," Owen told Jo.

"I didn't know."

But, of course, this was the Golden Oldies' Club, not the blow your own trumpet club.

"It's good of people to take the time," said Sharon. "I think Melanie started that. She was lovely."

A silence fell.

For Jo, any mention of Go Club co-founder Melanie came across in a similar way to talk of Victoria who retired before Bonner's moved to Avalon House. Both were legends familiar to others, but for Jo, they were somewhat mystical figures.

"Not long till the charity walk then," said Sharon.

"It's a great cause," said Jo.

"Make sure you harass and cajole everyone you meet, won't you. Every penny we raise goes a long way."

"I will."

But Jo hadn't thought of that. Harassing and cajoling people wasn't her thing.

"In a nice way," Sharon added. "The man in the corner store always pledged a fiver. Then I'd flutter my eyelashes and lower my voice, telling him what a fabulous chap he was. I'd walk out of there with a tenner promised every time."

While Sharon chuckled softly at the memory, Jo tried to imagine fluttering her eyelashes at the impassive block of ice who ran her local newsagent's. It didn't seem a likely game-changer.

"Don't forget to use your own skills," said Sharon. "If eyelashes aren't your thing, try something else. Logic and reason might do it. It's all about giving it a go."

"I'll try."

"Now Owen, you haven't given me the latest news from the allotment."

"Right, well, the latest is we have a mystery digger. It's either a bored retired coal miner, or a rabbit has found a way in. Investigations continue."

"I reckon it's the coal miner," said Sharon with a wink to Jo.

Owen went on to update her with news of fruit and vegetable harvests, and brief details of some local conservation activities in the wider area.

Once Sharon had digested his report, she turned to Jo.

"So… how are you enjoying retirement?"

"Oh, it's fine."

"Still finding your feet?"

"Yes, but I'm getting there… you know… onward and upward."

She wouldn't mention returning to Bonner's.

"I retired seven years ago," said Sharon. "I was a teaching assistant, and I loved it. I have to say I struggled to find anything meaningful to do during that first year away from work."

"But it turned out okay?"

"Eventually, yes. I'm no expert, but I think you have to say goodbye to your old life. Until then, you can't really move on."

Jo mulled it over. "That does make sense."

"I suppose it's easier if you hated your old job."

"I loved being at work."

"Then you loved being part of something, of having that sense of purpose. For you, leaving it behind is probably more like a death."

"A death?" Jo almost shivered.

"Yes, your old life is dead. You need a period of grieving for what was."

This talk of death made Jo felt uncomfortable.

"Oh, don't be too sensitive," said Sharon, picking up on Jo's unease. "I've had a wonderful life. But your time at work is over. You have to say I really enjoyed being there, but it's done. If you feel a sense of loss, then grieve for what's gone. Don't bury your emotions under a ton of pointless hobbies. Let the loss work its way out of you. Then, in time, you'll be free to move on."

Jo nodded.

Eventually, the conversation petered out and it was time to leave. The visitors did so with a dash of upbeat energy and a promise to pop in again soon.

Outside, they breathed in the summer air.

"Sharon mentioned Melanie," said Jo.

"Yes, one of our founders."

"It reminded me of Victoria who worked for Bonner's before my time. A legend and yet some of us never knew her. Whatever we do, no matter how great, our time comes and goes."

"Yes, Melanie, Victoria, you, me... even the fossils once had their day. That's why we have to make the most of life while we can."

Jo shrugged.

"So where does that leave us, Owen?"

25

One for the Park

On a glorious Sunday morning, Jo strolled through the gates of Tolcombe Park and down to the pond. There were families with brightly dressed young children everywhere. It was a lovely sight. Some days, it didn't feel so long ago that she was young on mornings such as this.

She recalled bringing her son, William, here to play on the swings. And didn't old Mr Bonner say his daughter Julia used to run riot around the pond years before William's time?

She passed a young dad playing ball with a toddler. Mum and a slightly older child were waiting thirty feet away for the ball to come to them.

"Enjoy every moment," Jo advised Dad. "They grow so fast."

He smiled. "Thanks, we will. It's what everyone tells us."

Jo smiled back at him and the toddler.

Yes, because it's true.

But old Mr Bonner was in her thoughts. She couldn't be sure if he was still alive. There hadn't been any news on that over the years – although, admittedly, contact had been lost long ago. Was he still around? If so, he'd be ninety, but that wasn't impossible these days.

By the pond, she sat on one end of a bench. The other end was occupied by a young jogger who had removed a training shoe to dislodge a small stone. She watched him refit the shoe and tie the laces. He was off and running again in no time.

Young people… she admired their energy.

She was being energetic too. She had decided to embrace retirement to the maximum before going back to work. Saturday had seen her do the regular trip to the supermarket. But shopping hadn't been joyless. Thanks to her new determination, she had stopped and talked to people while getting all the ingredients for spaghetti with spinach and goat's cheese.

The cooking itself went okay and she would have eaten it had Eddie not turned up. It took an hour and two cups of coffee to reassure him that his life wasn't over. She even mentioned the Go Club, but he scoffed at interfering types. When he finally left, she sat down and stared at a cold pasta… and then made a cheese toastie.

But that was yesterday.

A duck on the water flapped its wings before settling down again. Maybe that was her, stretching her wings but not flying just yet.

Of course, this was where she met them. The Go Club. That first time with them in silly costumes. The dragon, the pirate, Big Ben…

She couldn't speak for all older people, but for some, the next relationship was too important to get wrong. For some it was no doubt best to not go there, to protect oneself from potential hurt or embarrassment, to avoid having to admit that they should have known better.

Two young women walked by on the path by the bench. They were discussing an impending job interview.

Jo smiled and thought of her own interview at Bonner's forty years ago. Avalon House was new back then with fresh, clean concrete walls and shiny white window frames. She recalled the smell of disinfectant in the ladies' room while she checked her makeup... and the interview room at the end of the third-floor corridor. That was a storeroom these days. The interview panel was made up of Mr Bonner, Penny from Personnel, and Dennis, the man who would be her section head for the next two years. They asked questions about her filing skills and whether she could reach high shelves. Then came the wait to see who they had chosen... and the thrill of success.

Bonner's forty years ago. The people...

All gone.

But what of old Mr Bonner, who founded the company in the late 1960s, fifteen years before she joined?

She pulled her phone from her pocket and googled him. There wasn't much and none of it was useful. The company records weren't much use either as he sold the business in 2007 to a larger marketing outfit who retained the A. J. Bonner name for reputational and continuity reasons.

But his daughter, Julia. Three or four years younger than Jo, she tied the knot with an Irishman from Dublin sometime in the mid-nineties.

And the married name Julia Bonner took?

Yes, she knew it.

26

Mr. B

"It's just up here," said the cab driver as they made their way along a leafy street on the northern fringe of Bournemouth.

It had taken less than a minute to recall Julia's married name – Delahunty. And it didn't take any longer to find her on Facebook. Julia didn't recall Jo, but she was pleased that an old friend of her dad was taking an interest.

"Here we are – Primrose Lodge," said the driver as the five-mile trip from Jo's house came to an end at a residential complex.

Was this a good idea? She had phoned ahead and spoken to the manager. Everything was arranged. But what if he didn't remember her? Or what if he did but wasn't all that bothered about seeing her?

She paid the driver and, a moment later, pressed the entry buzzer.

There was a short wait before the young, male duty manager came to the door.

"Sorry about that…. I was helping someone."

"Oh, no problem. I rang earlier about Mr Bonner."

She couldn't bring herself to call him Alexander. It didn't feel right.

"Yes, come through."

She followed him to the reception desk, where she had to sign in. Then he took her into a communal lounge with an upright piano and a wall-mounted TV showing an old episode of Family Fortunes. There were three or four residents in comfy wingback chairs, although none were watching the screen.

Jo wondered – was this her own future? Didn't most retirees end up in a place like Primrose Lodge?

One resident, a man possibly in his nineties, caught Jo's attention. The blank stare, as if whatever was important to him was taking place in another reality.

"Just outside to the right," said the duty manager.

Jo thanked him and stepped out onto a patio with tables, chairs, and potted plants. Beyond it, a beautifully maintained lawn and shrub borders provided plenty of strolling space.

Initially, she couldn't locate him among the faces of residents and visitors. Her last sighting of him would have been… she tried to pinpoint it. The millennium? Yes, there had been a millennium bug with the potential to knock out computers when the date changed from 1999 to 2000. She couldn't recall why, and certainly nothing happened, but it had been Mr Bonner's final flurry of activity. Once all was deemed well, he stepped down and retired to Spain. Only, he was back home now, or at least not far from the huge, detached house he'd lived in during the eighties and nineties.

Then she spotted him. At least, she hoped so.

"Mr Bonner?"

An elderly man sitting alone at a round table squinted up at her but said nothing.

"Hello, Mr Bonner. It's Jo Ramsey. I called ahead."

"Yes?"

"Do you remember me? We worked together for almost twenty years."

"Yes... I remember."

"Oh great."

She sat down with him.

"It's lovely to see you, Mr Bonner."

"Yes... my, my... Jo..."

"It's been a while, hasn't it."

"Yes... a while."

"This is a really nice place. How long have you been a resident?"

"Oh... a while."

"The staff seem very friendly."

"Yes, well... they are. I loved my place in Spain, but..."

"Yes, well... you're back home in Bournemouth now. All the familiar sights. I remember when you lived near Meyrick Park."

She knew it to be a lovely area not far from the town, beach, and pier.

"Elizabeth and I had that place for forty years."

"That's a long time."

"Thing is, I need a bit of help these days."

"I suppose most of us do at some point."

"How's the firm?" he asked.

"Oh... they've moving soon, although I expect you already know that."

"No, I don't." He seemed agitated. "Where to?"

"A new place called Skyline. It's not too far from here, actually... a little farther west. Bonner's will have a whole unit to themselves."

"Makes sense, I suppose," he said, calming down again. "I expect I must have fallen off their contact list."

"It won't be the same as Avalon House, that's for sure."

"That's the way of the world. Avalon House wasn't anything like Logan Place."

"No, I suppose not."

Victorian Logan Place, 20th Century Avalon House, 21st Century Skyline. It was progress, she supposed.

"Did you work there?" he asked.

"Logan Place? No, I joined the company just after the move."

"Hmm… I'm sure you heard all the stories, but Logan Place was special."

Jo wondered about that.

"Was it though, Mr Bonner? Was Logan Place itself special, or was it just where you got the business off the ground?"

"There was a different spirit there. Yes, obviously, we were getting something going, but Logan Place had character. I used to love working in that old courtyard…"

He seemed to be reliving it, but for Jo, yet again, it was a reminder of her first days with the firm and the in-crowd who made Avalon House newcomers feel they had missed out. But she understood it. All kinds of places are special to all kinds of people. Life at Avalon House might have begun as sterile, but it developed over the decades. So many friendships had stretched to five, ten, fifteen years. One lasted seventeen.

"Do you remember Victoria?" he asked.

"I never worked with her, but I know she was a legend in the early days."

"She practically ran the place. If there wasn't a rule to cover it, she'd invent one – and that rule would become company law. When you watched her in action, it was like witnessing three people, because you couldn't work out how she covered so many situations. In some ways, you were like her."

Jo was taken by surprise. It sounded like a compliment. "I worked with Bessie for a while."

"Ah, Bessie. Poor lass. She used to take work home to get it finished. She hated the new technology…"

"Did she? She never said."

"She wouldn't use the new computers. We thought it would pass, but no. She was already in her sixties and had a blindness to technology."

"Now you mention it, she did spend most of her time dealing with people on the phone."

"She started work at fourteen during the War. She wasn't about to embrace a new age in the 1980s."

"She took me under her wing. My first few years were spent being made a fuss of, as if I were a long-lost daughter."

"Yes, and you were doing all her computer duties."

"Yes… now you mention it… I was."

Jo recalled the aftermath of Bessie's retirement. A dozen or more promised to visit her. But that first visit came six weeks later, and only five went to lunch with her. Six months later, a second visit was proposed – only diaries couldn't be synched, so it was abandoned. After nine months, two ex-colleagues eventually joined Bessie for lunch, but Jo wasn't one of them. And then, in a flash, another year had gone by and no one had made the effort.

Once in the early 1990s, Jo saw her in a supermarket in Bournemouth. She was dishevelled, reeked of alcohol, and was buying budget vodka. Jo slipped away without making contact.

"Is there something we can do together, Mr Bonner?" she asked. "A little walk, perhaps?"

"No, but… two things…"

"Yes?"

"Please call me Alex, and how are you at crosswords?"

Calling him Alex would be difficult, but…

"I'm not too bad at crosswords… Alex. Do you have one handy?"

"On the table there."

She leaned across to an unattended copy of Puzzles Monthly on the empty table next to them and flicked through to the first available fresh crossword. The clues looked user-friendly.

"Okay, ready?"

"Ready."

"One across… an ancient formation on Salisbury Plain. Ten letters."

"Stonehenge."

"I reckon you're right."

She penned it in.

"But how did they get the stones there?" he wondered aloud. "Have you seen the size of them?"

"I remember an admin assistant called Glenn who believed it was aliens."

"Glenn? When was he with us?"

"He would have been there around the early nineties. He worked under Don and had a fling with a copywriter called Vanessa."

"I remember Vanessa. Wasn't she the one who did show-jumping at weekends?"

"That's right."

"Okay, two across – composer of the opera, 'The Marriage of Figaro'…"

"Mozart!" said Alex. "I saw it at the Royal Opera House in London. That would have been… oh, sometime in the eighties. I remember having a business meeting in the City and thinking why not make a few days of it. My wife and I stayed at a hotel in Park Lane. Not sure which one, but they served cocktails with such a kick…"

Over the next hour or so, memories and laughs far outnumbered answers to crossword questions, and Alex Bonner very much came to life. However, Jo was all too aware of his great age, so the time to leave couldn't be put off forever.

"It's been lovely seeing you again," she said, squeezing his hand across the table. "I can't believe we only got through ten clues."

"Best crossword I've done in ages," he replied.

Her curiosity was satisfied. They could say their goodbyes.

But…

Some invisible force was tugging at her.

"Mr Bonner… Alex… shall I come and see you again?"

His eyes lit up.

"That would be lovely, Jo. Yes, thank you."

She felt a surge of enthusiasm.

"Are you busy Thursday afternoon?"

"Ooh, I'm sure there's a space in my diary."

"I'll phone before I come – see if you need any bits from the shops."

He smiled.

"Bless you, Jo."

She wished him well once more and left – her footsteps somehow lighter than on arrival.

Outside, she paused. Connecting with people felt good.

And then she thought – why not?

It was time for something she had never done before. She would invite people over to her place for dinner. And it would be Tuesday night.

Would anyone come?

She continued on her way feeling both nervous and excited.

27

Yum!

Standing in the quiet supermarket aisle, Jo studied the upmarket pack of spaghetti in her hand. It was more than twice the price of the supermarket's own brand, but how did they differ? Was upmarket spaghetti handmade by the Italian aristocracy and delivered by unicorns pulling golden wagons?

She read the back of the pack. The best coarse durum wheat semolina... better cooking performance... better sauce retention ... gluten integrity... firmness maintained after cooking... over a century of know-how...

Jo was into her third Tuesday of retirement – the longest time she had ever spent without having any work to do. It wasn't lost on her that Martin barely made it into his fourth week before keeling over in the hallway. She hoped her return to Bonner's next week wasn't being influenced by that in some hidden way.

Of course, the Bonner's connection had proved useful, with pledges of a fiver apiece from Jennifer, Annette, Amy, and three others in support of the charity walk. She would add twenty from her own pocket to make it a nice round fifty.

More immediately, Ruth, Marilyn, and Yvonne would be coming to dinner later. Delia and Alan had made their excuses. As for Owen, he wouldn't be there either as he had a prior engagement with an old actor friend in Bournemouth.

She refocused on the expensive spaghetti in her hand. With another crack at carbonara in mind, she placed it in the trolley.

"Right, so…"

She surveyed her haul thus far. Flowers for the vase, fresh fruit, veg, and herbs – consulting Owen on that would have been too complicated – frozen tempura prawns, desserts, cheeses, paper napkins, fragrant candles, everything for pasta carbonara…

She checked her list for the remaining items.

Chocolates, sparkling water, and wine.

Just then, Owen texted. She was both surprised and pleased that he'd made contact. They were fellow Go Club members, after all.

'Sorry, I can't be there later. Perhaps another time.'

She hesitated a little and then texted back.

'Yes, definitely.'

She didn't know what 'another time' might involve but guessed it would make sense to be prepared should it suddenly turn into dinner at her place in the coming days.

Staring at a million packs of pasta, Luca's words came back to her. Pasta alla Norma and roasted green beans. If Owen came round sooner rather than later, they'd have that. And if he didn't, she would get to enjoy Norma and beans by herself.

Pleased to have come up with a plan, she googled the recipes on her phone and set about hunting down the ingredients.

*

Jo beamed with pride as Ruth, Yvonne, and Marilyn took their seats at a beautifully laid table in the kitchen-diner. In the background, a soothing Mozart piano sonata added a touch of class – courtesy of a new smart speaker she'd bought on Monday at the mall.

"This is lovely," said Ruth.

"Yes, it is," said Marilyn. "What's on the menu?"

She didn't want them googling it and second-guessing her moves.

"It'll be a surprise."

"Ooh, lovely," said Yvonne. "I like to allow myself one day a week where I ease up on calorie counting – and it's today!"

"Then you've come to the right place," said Jo.

She had never felt like this at the Thursday after work drinks sessions and was beginning to get a sense of a potential new Jo, or perhaps a Jo who had never fully emerged. Certainly, her younger self had been more adventurous before life imposed its boundaries. Was that Jo resurfacing now?

She took it all in. Cooking for friends, relaxing music, a glass of wine…

Wine!

"Do open some wine, Marilyn."

She wanted to look like a chef, chopping and cooking while her guests enjoyed themselves at the table. She glanced at her mum, smiling at her from 1963.

Wish me luck.

Making a carbonara would be straightforward this time. The recipe was for four and she would follow it to the letter. *And* she would make sure the pasta was the correct temperature when she added the eggs.

"Is cookery a new hobby?" asked Marilyn.

"I hope so. The other things I tried weren't for me, but this feels… I can't explain it. Even if things go a little wrong, I'm looking to learn from it."

"I love passion," said Yvonne.

"Well, I'm just a beginner, but do hope something comes of it."

Ruth's words came back to her. To become a full member, she had to do something crazy for herself, something worthwhile for charity, and something wonderful for the community.

"I was thinking this might be the crazy thing I do for myself. For someone who has no track record in cookery, I might become an accomplished home chef."

"Good idea," said Ruth.

"You go for it," said Yvonne. "And we'll eat anything you need to road test."

"It'll take time," said Jo.

"That's something you have," said Marilyn.

As the conversation switched to Sunday's charity walk, Jo started the preparation by following the recipe on her phone.

Soon the pancetta was sizzling in the frying pan. Possibly sizzling a little too long, as peeling and chopping the garlic while joining in with the conversation was hardly an efficient way to get a meal ready.

While they discussed costumes old and new, and potential costumes for future events, Jo placed the spaghetti into the large pot of boiling water.

Next, they discussed ideas for a unified approach to costumes, whereby they might all be Flintstones, Star Wars stormtroopers, or dinosaurs – which Yvonne thought most appropriate.

Jo laughed along before switching to shaving the cheese onto a plate and washing the chives and parsley.

Only, for some reason, the pasta was already done.

She drained it and left it in the pot. It wasn't a problem. If the pasta was too hot, she would have pasta with scrambled eggs. Letting it cool a little was intelligent cooking.

Now all she needed to do was pick off the parsley stalks... which took about nine hours, or at least it felt like it – especially when the conversation turned to European travel and food.

But Jo could only stare at the growing horror in front of her. The stupid pasta was getting cold long before she was ready for it.

Yes, she could have chopped everything well in advance of dinner. But the cooking was meant to be part of the entertainment. She supposed now, it *would* be part of the entertainment when she told them there was no dinner.

Pizza delivery?

No!

If only she could stop all the swearing inside her head and concentrate. Or would swearing out loud add to the entertainment?

Get a grip, Jo...

Okay, so the hot pasta had to cook the raw egg. That was how it became a creamy dish. However, she no longer had hot pasta, but something resembling a cold mattress. It was a toss-up whether to eat it or put it outside for the birds to use as a trampoline.

Options, options...

Okay, could she cook more spaghetti?

No, because she had used it all up.

What about the rigatoni for the potential meal with Owen?

She wasn't sure. Rigatoni was a different kind of pasta – chunky tubes designed to fill up with sauce. But there was no sauce with carbonara. What if raw egg filled the rigatoni instead? Could she use a thin paint brush to clean the inside of each tube?

I'm a cook not a plumber.

By now, she had no idea what anyone was discussing at the table, nor did she care.

She glanced at Mum.

What do you think? Make something else?

What might she get away with? Lasagne? Spag bol? Or was it time for Norma to make an earlier than expected appearance? Undoubtedly, this was turning into a dramatic production.

Please don't notice me cooking a second meal.

She switched the oven on, took a gulp of wine, and got the recipe up on her phone. Apparently, pasta alla Norma was proof that simple ingredients could deliver stunning results.

Thankfully, she'd had the foresight to keep any cooking for Owen to a minimum as she didn't want 'entertainment' hampering any potential progress. Hence her having bought a pot of microwavable tomato sauce, and a garlic flatbread. All she had to do now was cut the two aubergines into rounds and bake them in the oven for thirty minutes.

"More wine?" she suggested to her guests.

"Yes!"

She took another bottle of malbec from the small rack on the side cabinet and handed it to Marilyn.

"Dinner will be half an hour, but I cheated and bought some tempura prawns for starters. They'll be ready in fifteen minutes."

"Hooray"

*

"This looks fantastic," said Ruth, as Jo placed a large, full pasta serving bowl on the table.

"Our surprise dish," said Yvonne.

"Yes, that's exactly what it is," said Jo.

Even to me.

"What's it called?" Marilyn asked.

"Ladies, say hello to… pasta alla Norma."

The story of its name could wait. She was too exhausted. Instead, she served up four portions and placed the cut garlic bread on a plate for all to share.

"This is wonderful," said Marilyn, tasting the sauce. "Are you sure you haven't been cooking Italian for years?"

"No, I've watched it on TV for years, but it's all new to me, cooking-wise. I thought I might concentrate on Italian first. Really get to know it, kind of thing."

"Mmm, I love Italian," said Yvonne. "What else will you be cooking?"

"Well… what do you guys like?"

"Lasagne," said Marilyn.

"Meat balls," said Yvonne in a growly, suggestive voice. "The juicier and meatier the better…"

"Carbonara," said Ruth, cutting Yvonne off.

"Ah yes, carbonara," said Jo. "I've never actually eaten it."

Cooked it twice, but…

"You remind me of me," said Ruth.

Jo was intrigued. "How so?"

"I wasn't one for action until recently. Now I occasionally throw the doors open to let a little more of life in. I got that from Melanie. When she passed away, I was ready to go back into my shell. But something stopped me. I'm not sure what, but I felt a new spirit rising in me. I thought – why not be a little more like Melanie? From that moment on, I've made every effort to keep the Go Club active, to keep having fun, and to keep enjoying life."

"So, my cookery passion… go for it?"

"Yes, broaden those horizons and believe in yourself. Also believe that life will find a way of adapting around you. What's the worst that can happen?"

"Burnt pans?" said Yvonne.

"I do feel something developing in me," said Jo. "In many ways, it's always been there, at least it was when I used to help my mum in the kitchen."

"Then go wild," Yvonne added. "Unleash the beast!"

Jo laughed.

"The only thing I'm about to unleash is… another bottle of wine."

"Hooray!" yelled Yvonne and Marilyn.

Ruth simply smiled.

While Jo retrieved Marilyn's malbec from the worktop, she considered Ruth. So, she had come out of her shell a little and was happier for it. That was great. Jo, herself, didn't feel too far inside a shell, but until recently she had felt devoid of vision. Now she could see more clearly.

Of course, Ruth had Alan. Only they never saw him. *Better not go there…*

The conversation continued to flow for the next half hour before a consensus arose that it was time to liberate the dessert.

"It's Sicilian lemon cheesecake," Jo announced.

A collective cheer went up.

"I cheated again though. I wasn't going to attempt making one this early into my cooking adventure."

"Next time then," said Ruth.

"Yes… next time…"

28

I Once Was Lost

Butterflies and bees were busy in the wildflower strip outside the walls of the hospice grounds. Perhaps in tune with all this summertime activity, Jo, Marilyn, Yvonne, and Delia were upbeat as they paid off the cab and passed through the gates.

Ruth, who lived ten minutes away on foot, was waiting by the main entrance, and was no less cheery when she spotted them.

"Right then..." she said.

Once again, in contrast to the fabulous sunny afternoon outside, the interior of the building was cool, while voices, raised outside, fell to just above a whisper.

Reaching Sharon's room, they found her sitting up in bed. She looked tired, but as usual, she rallied on seeing familiar faces.

It occurred to Jo just how alone Sharon was in life, and how much she cherished these get-togethers.

"No Owen, I'm afraid," said Yvonne. "He's either starring in a Hollywood blockbuster or he's gone to see his grandchildren in London. I can't quite remember which, but I know it was a fair excuse."

"He texted," said Sharon, her voice sounding more fragile than last time. "He mentioned two little monsters jumping on him and luring him to a secret camp – so it could be either."

Jo smiled along with the others but had only learned of Owen's trip via Marilyn.

"I have a request," said Sharon. "You won't know this, Jo, but when I was young, I was a regular in the choir."

"Me too," said Jo, the childhood memory stirring. "It's been a while though."

"Well," said Sharon. "I have an itch that needs scratching – to sing again. Do you think you could all be in the choir with me?"

The response was immediate and affirmative, although adult Jo had never been one for singing in public, unless when plastered at her own retirement party.

"You probably know the words," said Sharon, "but I got the nurse to print them anyway."

She indicated a couple of sheets of A4 on top of a chest of drawers.

Marilyn picked them up.

"Amazing Grace," she said, handing one of the sheets to Ruth and Yvonne.

Jo would share with Marilyn but she was concerned for their visually challenged friend.

"Delia, are you able to see this?"

Delia waved the sheet away.

"I think I can be relied on to know the words."

"Shall we then…" said Ruth.

"Go for it," said Yvonne.

Throats were cleared and Ruth led them off.

'Amazing grace, how sweet the sound,
That saved a wretch like me.
I once was lost, but now am found,
Was blind, but now I see.'

Jo's voice, quiet at first, gradually gained in confidence to match the others in covering for Sharon. It was a far cry from singing along with the Beatles and the Stones a few weeks back on a gallon of prosecco.

Her respect for the Golden Oldies' Club also grew. What they accomplished week in, week out absolutely had as much purpose as anything she had ever done in forty years at Bonner's.

The recital had barely finished when Yvonne brandished a piece of paper.

"Just a quick poem I jotted down."

"Ooh, I love Yvonne's poems," said Sharon, her voice now shot.

"You might want to cover your ears," Ruth advised Jo.

"There was a young woman from Venus, who could never get quite enough – just kidding. Ahem…"

'To be young again, to be free once more,
To revisit first love, to go wild for sure.
To see, to feel sensations sublime,
Everything, everything, that very first time.
Yellow for promise, red for passion, but oh…
Here come the blues.
No matter, there's hope if that's what we choose.
No longer young, we've worked through our plan,
For now, we continue… as best we can.'

Yvonne gave a little curtsey.

"That's lovely," said Sharon. "Thank you."

"I can do the rude one now, if you like?"

"Unfortunately, your time is up," said Delia. "Now let me recite something that was much loved by myself and my husband, God rest his soul."

Yvonne dutifully stepped back as Delia launched into Elizabeth Barrett Browning. 'How do I love thee? Let me count the ways…'

*

Half an hour later, they were back outside in the sunshine.

"She didn't look too bad," said Yvonne.

Nobody responded.

"Well, I'd best be off," said Ruth. "It's been lovely to see you all."

"I'm walking too," said Jo, leaving Marilyn, Yvonne, and Delia to wait for the return cab.

"I love our members," said Ruth as they strolled out through the gates. "To see them give so much really is special. They're making a difference almost every day of their lives. But they're not superhuman. We've been hoping to attract more retirees who can make a difference. You once said you believed every one of us should do our best. Maybe it's you we've been waiting for."

But Jo wasn't ready. There were other factors to consider.

"I'm heading off this way," she said at the junction. "I'll see you again soon, Ruth. Definitely."

Attempting to clear her head, she made her way down to the main road. Life was throwing up possibilities and she needed time. Thinking about Ruth and Sharon and Yvonne and Delia, she crossed the road and headed for the riverside path. This gave her a few minutes of solitude until she had to divert away through avenues of bungalows and then down a footpath to Park Street. Here, she passed the Bubble & Squeak café and the Crusty Cob bakery. A little farther along, she slowed.

No rush…

There was a touch of nervousness, a hint of anxiety – none of which made any sense. Even at the door of the Red Lion, she hesitated. She just needed a moment to shift her mindset away from the Go Club.

She pushed the door open. It was noisy and lively and smelled of beer and unidentifiable hot food. Then, from two tables pushed together in a corner, heads turned, and a small cheer went up.

It was such a familiar scene.

She gave a little wave and went to join Annette, Amy, Kim, Jennifer, and Nina. Terry was also there. That was fine though. Most bosses could never come to this kind of drinks meetup, but Terry knew how to switch off. And he'd always be generous when getting his round in.

As it was, he grabbed his bottle of beer, and got up.

"Let me get you a drink, Jo." He was indicating that she should join him at the bar. "It's good to see you. What can I get you?"

"Any zero lager, please."

He ordered one from the barman.

"You'll really be helping us, Jo. Bonner's needs you."

"That's very kind of you to say."

"It's going to be a bit of a bumpy ride as we make the transition. It looks like we're losing a few, and we'll have half a dozen coming in as part of an expansion."

The barman placed a chilled bottle and a glass on the bar and Terry tapped his debit card on the reader.

"I need people I can rely on. People I can trust. People who care. People like you and Jennifer. Did you know she's staying on?"

"Yes, she mentioned it."

"We've got some huge new projects – an ocean science initiative, another homeless one, and one about healthcare in North Africa. I don't want anyone dropping the ball."

"Busy times then."

"More than busy, Jo. This is our hour of need. I knew you wouldn't let us down. Besides, you'll love it at Skyline."

She nodded, although perhaps without full-on enthusiasm.

Terry picked up on it.

"I'm serious. You'll be on the second floor at the back. It has big windows looking out onto open countryside."

"Sounds good."

But would she be happy peering out at open countryside and not walking through it?

He clinked his bottle against hers.

"Cheers, Jo. Good to have you back."

"Thanks."

But was coming back a good thing? Did it make sense? She thought about it as she and Terry returned to the pushed-together tables to sit with the others.

Yes, it *was* a good thing. They needed her and she would have a job packed with structure and purpose. *And* she would restart her friendships with Jennifer, Annette, and Amy.

On the downside, she'd be working more closely with moaner Kim.

"So, what have you been up to?" Amy asked as Jo poured the bottled beer into the glass. "Last I heard it was pottery."

Pottery felt like a million years ago.

"No, that wasn't for me. Neither was the art class nor the reading group at the library."

"Sounds like the call from Bonner's came just in time," said Annette.

"Well, I've met some nice people. They've become friends."

"That's great," said Amy. "You have plenty of friends who miss you at work, of course."

"Thanks. It's nice to be here again."

"Have you missed us?"

"Yes, of course I have. Cheers."

They all raised their drinks and Jo took a long, refreshing draught. Singing Amazing Grace with Ruth, Marilyn, Yvonne, Delia, and Sharon less than an hour ago seemed a world away.

"How are you getting to Skyline?" asked Jennifer.

"Um…"

"If you can be at my place by eight, you can come with me and hubby."

"That would be perfect. Thanks."

"I must tell you about our latest client," said Nina. "I'm in love."

"He's a charity fundraiser," Amy explained. "Animal welfare."

Jo smiled. She was wholeheartedly back in the fold. No secrets or non-disclosure agreements now. She was one of them again.

And yet…

"They have a regional base in Poole," said Nina, "so I'm going over there to discuss some aspects of the campaign."

"Completely necessary once you've clapped eyes on the client," said Annette. "Nina, you'll probably need to have dinner with him to get everything you need."

Kim and Amy smirked.

"On reflection," said Terry, "I think a zoom call might be the way to go for you on that one, Nina."

"Really? I don't mind paying my own cab fare."

"Yes, well, you'll be free to do that after the project's finished."

Nina mumbled something about the dishy guy heading to London once the project was over, but Jo became distracted by her phone ringing.

That was unusual.

She checked the screen.

"I must take this. Sorry."

"Ooh, secret lover?" Annette asked.

Jo stepped outside to answer.

"I didn't want to text," said Owen.

"That's okay. What is it?"

"I was wondering… would you fancy lunch tomorrow or over the weekend?"

He wasn't the only one wondering – would this be an up-close-and-personal lunch or a retirement advice lunch?

"Yes, okay – I'd love to. Tomorrow's fine for me."

"Tomorrow, okay, great. How does a picnic sound?"

"A picnic? Lovely."

"Great. Text me your address and I'll pick you up at, say, twelve-thirty…?"

"Okay."

"Perfect. I'll see you tomorrow then."

"Yes, tomorrow."

29

An Outing for Three

Resplendent in a pale-yellow blouse and sky-blue summer skirt, Jo waited at the living room window, which looked out onto the street. With the sun high overhead, she had also dug out a straw hat as she had no intention melting into the picnic blanket.

She was ready – at least, as ready as she ever would be for whatever kind of lunch date it might be. Although, just in case, she had sprayed a little of the Joyful Strawberry scent she received as a Secret Santa gift three years ago. It had never been opened so its tones were fruity and sharp.

As she watched the occasional vehicle go by, she daydreamed about how things might go, although rather than reach any kind of conclusion, she had to keep restarting her dream due to random catastrophes ruining things. Seriously, was their first kiss likely to be interrupted by an asteroid strike?

And suddenly, there he was – coming up the front path. She hurried to the door to welcome him.

"Good to see you, Owen."

"You too, Jo. All set?"

"Yes, all set."

"You look great, by the way."

"Thanks." Receiving compliments definitely took a little getting used to. "You look great too." And maybe handing them out needed some work. He did look good though in a smart short-sleeve sky blue shirt over light sand chinos.

"I have a confession, Jo," he said as she stepped out of the house and closed the front door behind her. "I need to tell you about someone else in my life. It's Miranda. She's in her late fifties but she still turns heads."

Jo was a little confused, and slightly taken aback. This was meant to be a lunch date.

Owen was smiling.

"It's time you met her."

Jo was still trying to form a reply when he showed her to a car parked across the street – an eye-catching 1960s vintage red Morris Minor with a cream soft top that had been retracted to reveal an impressively restored cream interior.

"May I introduce you to Miranda."

The confusion melted away. And she felt her eyes mist. Was it his gentleness?

Owen addressed the car.

"Miranda, say hello to Jo."

Jo felt like waving to Miranda but refrained.

"She's lovely. She really is. Is she a Morris?"

"Yes, a Morris Minor 1000. Thing is, she loves getting out. Seriously, this whole thing was her idea."

"A trip for three? It's a lovely idea."

"Brilliant. Now, don't be alarmed, but she can sometimes be a little slow to start."

"I know how she feels."

Owen's gaze turned serious. "She might be getting old, but once she gets going, there's no stopping her." Then his face broke into a grin. "We can keep the innuendo going if you like."

Jo laughed. A little silliness wasn't the worst way to pass a moment or two.

"I'll let you get your topless lady all revved up then."

He smiled generously as they got in.

"Right then, Miranda Morris…"

He turned the ignition. In response, Miranda had a little think about starting… and then let out a full-throated roar.

Jo felt excited. She would be heading into a new unknown. Okay, so not a mission to Mars, but going for a drive with Owen in a lovely old car called Miranda. An absolute certainly filled her heart – this kind of thing simply hadn't happened enough in her life.

"Ready?" he asked.

She fastened her hat strings under her chin.

"Ready."

A few minutes later, as they approached the junction that would get them across the High Street, Owen brought them to halt at a red light. A mother and young daughter were waiting for the pedestrian light to turn green while, on the opposite side, an elderly man was also waiting to cross.

It was only a few seconds, but in that moment, Jo experienced something wholly new and completely unexpected.

They're smiling at us!

She had sat with Martin in their car thousands of times, but no one had ever given them a second glance. Here, she found herself waving to the little girl and getting a wave back. Owen might not have been a leading actor, but Miranda Morris was an absolute star!

*

Twenty-five minutes later, they pulled into a quiet car park in the New Forest, not too far from the public conveniences, which Jo appreciated without saying.

"There's a clearing just through there," said Owen.

"Great," said Jo, relieved that the breeze in their faces while driving hadn't disappeared entirely. Here, it was coming through the trees bringing the essence of the forest with it. With a straw hat apiece and a few fluffy white cumulus clouds above, they had plenty of respite from the mid-June sun.

Once Miranda's top was up and her doors locked, Jo and Owen set off along a quiet trail deeper into the countryside – although they soon had to stop to say hello to some horses the other side of a fence. They also met a dog walker and made a new friend in Flossie the border collie.

Eventually, they came to a halt, both of them puffing a little.

"How about here?" Owen suggested. They were overlooking a tranquil clearing.

"It's perfect."

They unfolded their lightweight chairs and laid a blanket for lunch. The food could wait though while they sat and reset themselves. In fact, Jo found it so peaceful she wondered if they should speak at all.

But, of course, she wanted to get to know Owen better.

"You don't say much about being a television actor," she observed.

"Oh, I can show off with the best of them, if need be."

"I know people who do routine admin jobs and never stop going on about it."

"Admin's important. No admin, no smooth running of any organization."

"True…"

Her return to Bonner's crossed her mind but this didn't seem to be a good time to mention it.

"I do talk about times past," he said. "I'm proud of what I've achieved."

"It must have been hard to walk away."

"Yes, but it became tiring. Not so much physically, but psychologically. It's far more strain than you might think waiting for the email or phone call. I was no A-lister and my agent was hardly inundated with offers. You have to be realistic. I was never going to be happy getting older and chasing less and less work. Some do, of course, and I absolutely admire them."

Jo was sympathetic but didn't want to let him drift into negative emotional territory.

"How about we eat," she suggested.

The picnic was soon set out. A small cheese and onion quiche, mushroom rice salad, cherry tomatoes, coleslaw, green leaves, French bread, and a bottle of non-alcoholic prosecco.

"Tell me a bit more about Miranda," said Jo between mouthfuls. "When did you first set eyes on her?"

"About twenty years ago. She was shacked up with a guy in Bournemouth. I was lucky enough to have use of my parents' garage as they had just about given up trying to get their big Toyota in and out of it without scratching something."

"Is that where you're living now – at your parents' place?"

"Yes, I had enough money to buy a small flat, but I ended up staying there. It still feels like Dad's place. Not so much Mum's – she passed away quite a while ago."

Jo could readily empathise, but once again she wanted this to be an upbeat encounter.

"Are old cars like Miranda expensive?" she asked.

"Good question. You can get them dirt cheap, but they'll be in a terrible condition – which is how Miranda was when I found her. A lovely lady but definitely not at her best."

"And you restored her?"

"Mostly. I had help from Dad and the paint job is professional."

"She really is lovely. Would you ever sell her?"

"Oh definitely – every wintry morning when she refuses to start. We certainly have a few choice words then, but… well, what can you do when you're in love."

Jo laughed.

"It goes deep then."

"It does. A little while ago, a man from Brighton offered me twelve thousand for her."

"Oh wow, that's a lot of money."

"I thought about it, but Miranda looked at me with those big headlights, and smiled in that coy, polished grill way she has… it's not easy to divorce a Morris Minor."

"No, I can see that now."

"We belong to the Morris Minor Owner's Club. Lots of lovely get-togethers, rallies, restoration tips…"

"Morris Minor owners sound like a good bunch."

"Oh, we are. Although there are cruel owners. Those who buy cheap and try to skimp and cut corners. Right now, there are Mirandas, Myrtles, and Maxines out there being rubbed with harsh sandpaper. There really ought to be a law against it."

"Too right. Those poor ladies."

They drifted into a pleasant, comfortable silence and Jo tried to take it all in. The sun through the treetops. The gentlest of breezes. A lazy bee wafting by. Two walkers in the distance. A lone bird singing somewhere nearby.

When they started talking again, it became an hour and a half on everything and anything, from youthful escapades to places visited to more on Jo's years with Bonner's and Owen's backstage stories.

But all too soon, their time was up. Jo was a little disappointed. Had he produced a tent, she would have stayed all night. As it was, they packed up in good spirits and prepared to leave.

But time froze with them facing each other.

It was Owen who leaned forward to bridge the gap, his aftershave wafting pleasantly. And as their lips touched, she had to go back almost half a century to recall a kiss anything like it.

"Ready for home then?" he asked.

"Yes," she said, not wanting to go home at all.

"Right."

"What does the future look like?" she asked as they set off back to the car.

"Do you really want to know?"

"Yes."

"How are you fixed for this afternoon?"

Jo felt hope rising even though she wasn't sure what he meant.

"I'm free."

"It's just that I'm reading a play that may or may not become a local amateur production. It might work for me, it might not. You could help me with my lines. If you're interested?"

It wasn't quite what she'd had in mind, but it sounded intriguing.

30

Late in the Afternoon

Owen lived in a 1930s semi-detached house with an attached garage in a well-kept tree-lined street. It was the kind of place birds chose to live, judging by the avian singing competition currently in progress.

Having parked Miranda in front of the garage, he led Jo into the house and through to an outdated kitchen-diner at the back.

"Let's let some air in, shall we?" he said, opening the French doors.

She peered out onto a large garden with an ancient greenhouse full of young plants. The more mature plants – mainly herbs – were in various pots on metal stands spread around the patio.

"Tea, coffee, cold drink?"

"Water's fine, thanks."

"Same here."

She took a seat at the dining table while he went about getting their drinks.

"I can offer you some bread and jam too," he said, indicating half a French stick on the bread board, clearly left over from the picnic preparations.

"I'm fine, thanks."

He joined her at the table, sitting opposite.

"Okay, so, the play… you don't have to do it. It's entirely up to you."

"I'd like to help."

"Only if you're sure."

"I am."

"Great, thanks. I might not be looking for work these days, but I'd like to avoid going rusty."

"Understandable."

"So, I'm up for the role of Harry, the father. If you could read the other roles in my scenes, that would be very helpful. You don't need to act them, just read them straight. I'll act my lines, obviously."

"Okay, fine."

"Right, so, my entrance comes a few pages into Act One. If you could just read from there."

She turned the stapled sheets of A4 until she found the place.

"Shouldn't we read it from the start to get the pace?" she wondered.

"No need."

"Okay, but…"

"But?"

"Well… I worked in admin for forty years. One thing about my job was knowing all aspects of a project, including how we got to where we were."

He sized her up.

"Okay, if you insist."

"I'm no expert, but if a job's worth doing…"

"Then please go ahead."

"Right, so…" she returned to the opening and studied the directions on the page. "It starts with Christina and her boyfriend Daniel entering Harry's living room."

"Yes, my character, Harry, Christina's father, comes in on page four."

"Right… so, I'm both Christina and Daniel."

"Yes."

"And you'll join us on page four."

"Harry will, yes."

"Got it. So…" She cleared her throat. "I'll now be Christina and Daniel."

"Right."

She cleared her throat again.

"Perhaps a sip of water?" he suggested.

"No, I'm fine. Here goes. Ready?"

"Ready."

"So, it's Christina who speaks first."

"Yes."

"Right…"

"Go for it."

"Okay, so… I'm Christina and Daniel now. And I'll just read it straight through. Ahem…"

'Ah, home again. With the bonus of Dad not being here. Who says a girl can't get lucky?'

'Nice place.'

'You can tell your probation officer it'll be your home for the next few weeks. Until we can get you sorted.'

Jo suspected she sounded like a robot reading a grocery list, but she continued all the same.

'Are you sure your dad won't make a fuss?'

'Don't worry about him. You only need to focus on yourself. And me, of course.'

'You haven't forgotten? I've been locked up for six months.'

'No, I haven't.'

'I think it's affecting my priorities.'

'Oh, in what way?'

'Put your arms around me and I'll explain.'

'Like this?'

'Yes, like that. Do you know this is probably the most sensual moment of my life?'

Jo swallowed drily as her delivery became ever more mechanical.

'Oh Daniel.'

'Oh Chrissie…'

'Oh.'

'Oh.'

'Oh.'

'Oh.'

Jo became aware of a strange noise. It was Owen. His lips were clamped together and his shoulders were shaking. Was he having a fit?

"Owen?"

He recovered superbly, turning any hint of hilarity into a bout of coughing.

"Sorry, Jo. As you were."

"You mentioned your character coming in on page four. Shall we skip ahead to that?"

"Good idea."

"Obviously, I'm keeping any feelings out of the reading."

"Of course."

"I mean I'm aware the hatstand in your hallway displays more emotion, but that's what I'm deliberately going for."

"Absolutely right."

"So… the notes say Harry comes home to find his daughter waiting for him. His surprise and delight plummets into disappointment and annoyance when he sees Daniel on the sofa."

'Father, you're home. I was beginning to think you'd moved in with that woman. I can't quite recall her name.'

Owen sighed.

"Jo…"

"What? More emotion, or…?"

"No, I've decided I don't want to do it."

"The play?"

He was flicking through the pages.

"I don't think I can bring anything to it."

Jo felt bad.

"I hope this isn't my atrocious reading skills. I was doing my best."

"No, no – not at all. Please don't think that."

"Right, well…"

"I was hoping to share a wonderful experience with you but having the script open again… I know what's coming and it's just not for me."

"Are you sure?"

"I've read through it a few times – and seriously, it's nothing to do with your reading. I'm very grateful. Perhaps another time, another play. Something I can bring something to."

Jo tried to understand.

"So, what's wrong with it.?"

"Oh… things. For one, Harry says right out that he doesn't like Daniel. Yes, he's been in prison, but telling him on their first meeting that he doesn't like him… I might be wrong, but that kind of thing should simmer for longer. It's the niceties being strained to breaking point that creates the drama."

"Yes, I see." She put her copy down. "So that's that?"

"I'll send it back with a friendly note."

"You said you never turned anything down for television."

"That's different, I was a working actor. Every job in television has a split focus – the job in hand and the opportunity to network."

Jo gave a small smile.

"Are you *sure* my wooden acting didn't influence your decision?"

"Jo, your acting was pinpoint and incisive. You nailed it."

"So, you'd be happy to work with me again then?"

"Yes."

Her heart rate rose. She felt warm.

"But we'd do it for love, not money?"

Owen smiled. "Yes."

"Well… good. I'm glad."

"I've said it before but getting retirement right is so important." He nudged the script on the table. "This is all part of that process."

Jo knew the rest – that once you got retirement right, you would be in a good place to begin a relationship. But was he right?

"How was it when you first retired?" she asked.

Owen puffed out his cheeks.

"I struggled because I had no plan. Dad had just died and I was on my own. Then I met someone and things improved quite a bit – for a few weeks. Then we split up. My fault. I was trying to fix retirement with a relationship whereas she just wanted lunch one day, dinner another, and maybe trips to ancient monuments on Sundays – that kind of thing. After that, retirement was worse because I felt even more alone with nothing I cared about to look forward to."

She wanted to squeeze his hand across the table but refrained.

"For a few months, things got worse," he said. "But then one day I was waiting for the ferry and I started chatting with this extraordinary woman. She was going on about abstract expressionism and the works of Willem de Kooning."

"Yvonne?"

"Yes… and what was so engaging was her passion for painting. I don't share it, but it seemed to me, that's what I was missing. Anyway, it transpired that she belonged to a small group, completely unofficial, no memberships fees or forms to fill in, come as you please, take it or leave it. Well, I couldn't turn that down, could I."

"No, absolutely not. So that's how you joined the Go Club."

"Yes, it was Melanie, Ruth, Alan, Delia, Sharon, Mandy, Mitch, Yvonne and me. I haven't looked back since, and I don't intend to."

"I'm glad you found them."

She wanted to tell him of her impending return to Bonner's, but she couldn't find the words. For one thing, it would spoil the moment, and potentially spoil many more moments to come. She peered outside. The garden was a picture of summer tranquillity.

"I love late afternoon," she said.

"Are you talking about the time of day or where we are in life?"

She felt a smile tug at her cheeks.

"Yes, we're definitely in late afternoon territory. But that's okay. It's still a while till sunset."

"Right, well… on more practical matters, Miranda and I can offer you a ride home. She won't mind going to bed late. Or…"

"Or…?"

"I could offer you some tea or… well, I know it's only half-four, but I've a nice bottle of malbec in the rack."

Jo considered it. In the old days, hadn't this been a code for certain other activities? Was it still a code? Or did it just mean they would have a glass of wine?

"Oh, go on then. Wine."

"Are you sure?"

"No need for Miranda to go out past her bedtime. I can always get a cab."

"Right, well… great."

How would it be? Assuming it *would* be. She felt a little self-conscious.

Owen returned to the table with the bottle and two glasses.

"It's a good one. They had it on offer, so I got a couple of bottles."

A moment later, the screw cap was off and their glasses were half filled with a deep, warm, dark red wine.

"Cheers, Jo."

"Cheers to you too."

They clinked glasses and she took a sip. The pleasing warmth washed over her tongue and met the back of her throat. This was good wine.

"Mmm, lovely."

Sixty-eight years of age? All that experience? It didn't count. In truth, she felt a little unsure of herself.

"It's quite warm in here," he said.

Oh gawd... not the old "it's quite warm" ploy.

Not that she'd ever experienced it as a ploy. Maybe it wasn't a ploy. Maybe it was just quite warm. Or maybe she was sweating? How embarrassing. What was that old saying? 'Men sweat, ladies perspire.' Who said that? Should she google it?

She took a calming quaff of wine.

"Are you a fan of malbec?" he asked.

What was he on about now? Was he suggesting that she was glugging it too quickly?

"Mmm," she said, her mouth full of the stuff..

Her stomach rumbled.

Could he hear it?

Hear it? Next door probably think there's an earthquake.

"We might need to eat at some point," he said.

"Yes."

"I don't have much in though."

She thought for a moment. They had enjoyed a few tomatoes as part of the picnic. Had he bought a pack?

"Do you have tomatoes?" she asked.

"Er... yes, there's most of a fresh pack in the fridge."

"And basil?"

"In the greenhouse, yes."

"Olive oil?"

"Um... yes, I do have a small bottle in the cupboard."

"Black pepper?"

"Yes."

"Right, well, we'll cut the bread into slices and make bruschetta."

"Will we?"

"Yes."

"Have you done that before?"

"No, but I know we'll be very happy eating it."

Their eyes met but she couldn't hold his gaze for more than a couple of seconds.

"I'm a little old these days," she said, "and I'm not sure how this will go."

"Same here... but I'm fairly sure this is our time."

He reached across the table and took her hand in his.

"A few weeks ago, I wouldn't have expected this to happen," he said.

"Me neither. Do you think plans sometimes have a habit of going their own way?"

"Yes, I do. I have a feeling my plans and your plans have already met for a drink and swapped notes."

She smiled. "That's a funny idea."

"Are you sure you're not in a hurry to get home?"

Her heart thumped. "No, no hurry. My plans have just told me I have all the time in the world."

He got up and came around the table to kiss her softly on the lips.

She responded.

And in that moment, it was everything she wanted.

31

A Friend in Need

Light peeked around the edges of the drawn curtains. It was morning.

Last night!

It seemed impossible. Surely, age would have robbed her. But no.

Passion... intensity... her body fizzing with electricity...

"Good morning," whispered Owen.

She turned to face him.

"Hello."

"Sleep well?"

She smiled.

"Yes."

He raised himself onto an elbow so that he could nuzzle her neck. It felt so incredibly good, and different too. No one had ever done that before.

"I'm glad you stayed," he murmured.

"Me too."

He looked at her earnestly. "It wasn't so bad then?"

"It was… indeed not so bad."

He laughed and they kissed, soft and unhurried.

"Mmm," she uttered.

"Tea or coffee?" he asked.

"Tea, please."

As he sat up, she stretched her entire body.

"Come down when you're ready. We'll sit on the patio."

Owen got out of bed. A vision of naked male beauty? Well, no, his lurid tartan pyjamas had the situation covered.

"I might need sunglasses if you don't cover those up."

He grinned as he opened the curtains to let in a beautiful summer's morning. He then donned a dark blue dressing gown.

"Here," he said, placing a second dressing gown on the bed for her – this one charcoal.

A few moments later, she enjoyed hearing him downstairs clinking cups and a spoon while she luxuriated in bed.

"Are you happy, Jo?" she asked herself. "Yes, I am. Thanks for asking."

She got up and stretched again. Then she pulled on the dressing gown – which was a hundred sizes too big. But that was okay. It was Owen's, so it fitted perfectly if you factored in her being in love with life.

Yes, something had changed. It wouldn't be visible in a mirror, but a missing piece was now in place.

A short while later, on the patio, they were sipping tea and watching a robin splashing in the bird bath. But Jo was thinking ahead. How would the rest of the morning play out? What would they do?

"I'll drive you home after breakfast," said Owen, which frustratingly wasn't one of the scenarios she'd had in mind.

"Okay."

"I have an Open University essay to write."

"Oh right. Are you doing a degree?"

"Not quite – I was just rooting around their website and found some really good online courses. This one's a degree module, so I could use it towards gaining a degree at some point, but that's not the aim. I just fancied studying something interesting."

"What's the course?"

"It's 'The Environment in a Changing World', and the essay I'm fashionably late with is about cities and towns. Did you know the majority of the world's population is now urban?"

"No... although I've never really thought about it."

"We're studying how we can make cities and towns more resilient, liveable, and sustainable. I haven't had much time this past week and it has to be in on Monday morning."

"Ah right. And it's the charity walk tomorrow."

"Yep, Sunday's a write-off, but um..."

Jo sensed he wanted to say something important.

"About my daughter," he continued. "I've been thinking..."

"Yes...?"

"Holly, Jacob, and my grandchildren..."

"Jack and Abigail."

"Yes... maybe I don't need to relocate."

"Oh right." Jo's heart fluttered.

"I mean life here is good and I do see them a few times a year. Maybe I'm luckier than I realised."

"Yes... I suppose we can all realise that from time to time."

"So..."

"Yes, so... perhaps we could have dinner at my place sometime."

"I'd love to. Will it be Italian?"

"Definitely. And I'll make a dessert. How does tiramisu sound?"

"Fabulous. Tell me, what's in tiramisu? I know it's coffee…"

"Yes, and double cream, mascarpone, sugar, sponge fingers, and chocolate."

Owen laughed. "I'm putting on calories just thinking about it."

*

Jo was back at home, enjoying a cup of tea and issuing the occasional satisfied grin. The rest of the day would be about relaxation ahead of tomorrow's charity walk.

How things had changed.

Owen's take on the dangers of starting a relationship to patch over an unfulfilling retirement had initially shaken her. But they were past that point now. At least she believed so.

She understood something else too. Maybe not the answer to everything, but perhaps, finally, the right question.

Who was Jo Ramsey?

It seemed a silly thing to ask herself – at first. But was she a woman defined by working for Bonner's? Or was she something more? Because if the latter, perhaps she was beginning to see what 'something more' might look like.

Dinner with Ruth, Yvonne, and Marilyn came back to her. Despite the mini disaster, she had known there was something wonderful emerging from within. Yes, people would always be passionate about signing up for yoga or judo or amateur dramatics but, for her, this really did feel like the beginnings of a genuine passion, of a deeper curiosity, of a yearning to know more, and of a reconnection with the past.

There was something else too.

She'd been thinking if you can't go to Italy, then bring Italy to you – which was a great way to look at it. But now? She was thinking something very different, something much bigger. Who said she couldn't go to Italy…?

Her phone pinged. A text from Marilyn.

'Could you help with Yvonne? I'm tied up for a bit.'

She texted straight back. 'Yes.'

Further texts explained the situation. Yvonne had an appointment with a one-to-one mentor; someone she'd been seeing for the past two years. Only, she had let Marilyn know she wouldn't be going.

Jo phoned for a cab and used the fifteen-minute wait to change clothes. Marilyn, currently in a hair salon in Middle Tolcombe, would meet her at Yvonne's as soon as possible.

*

"You look nice and relaxed," said Yvonne, greeting Jo at the door.

"And you look…"

"Frazzled?"

"What's happened."

"I failed. I had a one-to-one and I didn't go."

"We all fail sometimes."

"Come in. I'll put the kettle on. Tea or coffee?"

Jo came in but only as far as the hall.

"Yvonne, are you sure it's too late? What time was the appointment?"

"Half an hour ago."

"They could be running late. How about we phone?"

"She'll be halfway through her next appointment."

"Yes, but we won't know unless we try."

Yvonne stared down at her feet. There was an air of disappointment about her.

"I watched Sleepless in Seattle again last night," she said. "Wouldn't it be nice to say I watched it with a boyfriend even though he's not into old rom-coms, but hey, that's boyfriends for you and the passion we shared afterwards was amaaaaazing. Do you think I'm weird?"

"No, you're lovely, and one day someone will see how great you are."

"Flatterer. And how about you? I heard you were with Owen?"

"Yes, a lunchtime picnic in the New Forest. It was lovely."

"Sounds fun. He's always made excuses to stay on his own."

"Yes, well…"

"I want the best for him, Jo. He's a friend."

"I know."

"Did you see him last night?"

"Er…"

"He was in a murder mystery on ITV4."

"Ah, right. No, I…"

Yvonne moved into the living room and switched the TV on.

"I recorded it. Don't worry, I'm not obsessed or anything. It was on at six, but I don't watch TV till around eight."

She began the playback and fast-forwarded through the first few minutes.

"Yvonne… we should probably be talking about your one-to-one."

"He only pops up three times."

"Yes, but…"

The first appearance was already on the screen.

"He plays a bloke in the pub who saw the main suspect acting suspiciously."

"Right…"

Owen not only looked younger, he looked different – although that might have been the bedraggled look of the character he was playing.

"Just think," said Yvonne. "If you were a super-fan, you could watch Owen through the ages. I think this one's from the mid-nineties."

It did seem odd, but then again, didn't most people have old photos and videos?

"I hope they're paying him royalties," she said.

"Oh, I'm sure he gets a few pennies to top up his pension."

Jo studied his performance, although there wasn't much more of it before the episode cut to a break.

"I'm glad he's over his struggle with retirement," said Yvonne. "He's in a nice groove these days. It looks like you're getting there too."

"Yes, although…" At that moment, she had a sudden, overwhelming desire to be honest with her friend. "I have a chance to return to work."

"Oh…" said Yvonne, the surprise all too evident in her eyes.

"It's only just come up."

She decided to skip over the fact she was due in on Tuesday to start a twelve-month contract.

"So," said Yvonne. "What will you do?"

"Um…"

The doorbell rang.

A moment later, Yvonne was showing Marilyn in and all three were swapping hellos. Any consideration of Jo's return to work was brushed aside by Marilyn getting down to the reason she and Jo were there.

"So, what happened?"

Yvonne puffed out her cheeks. "I failed."

"Okay, so you're at home when you should be having a one-to-one."

"I just couldn't face it."

"You're in a bad place right now. There's too much going on. It'll pass, okay? You remember a few months back? When I was in a bad place?"

"The gym on the High Street?"

"No, when I left Gavin for a few weeks."

"I remember. You were in a bad place. But it passed."

Jo was smiling encouragement at Yvonne while trying to process Marilyn's revelation.

"Yvonne, I'm trying to help," Marilyn prompted.

"I know. I'm sorry. You're my best friend and I love you and appreciate all your massive support. I just think this time it's beyond our joint powers. Unless you've acquired new powers? Like in that movie we saw last week?"

"It'll pass, Yvonne. Okay? It'll pass."

"I know but, seriously… have you acquired any new powers?"

"Yvonne… let me call your mentor. Have you got the number?"

A moment later, Marilyn was talking to a woman called Catherine.

"Yes, I'm with Yvonne now. She's just got back from helping me with an emergency… I fell and hurt my ankle. We didn't know if I'd need to go to the hospital, so she stayed with me. Anyway, I'm fine but Yvonne has wrecked her own schedule."

Jo crossed her fingers and smiled at Yvonne.

"Yes... yes..." Marilyn continued. "That would be brilliant... yes, I'll see she gets there. Well, obviously not me. I've got an ankle thingy... yes, yes, great. Bye."

Marilyn ended the call.

"How's the ankle?" Yvonne asked.

"Never mind that, she's pushed back a client and is cutting her lunch break. She'll give you forty minutes if you can get there right away."

"Um...?"

"Yvonne, please, we need to be there as soon as possible."

"Okay, I got this."

Yvonne went off to get ready.

"Do you think she'll ever get back to her fighting weight?" Jo wondered.

"I have absolutely no idea," said Marilyn, "but we'll never give up and leave a friend alone to struggle."

32

The Charity Walk

Eddie? On her sofa? How?

"Would you do something for me?" he asked. "It's quite personal."

"What?"

"Would you... do my laundry? It's only a couple of bags."

Argh.

Her eyes sprung open.

It was Sunday morning and she had overslept. That was okay though. To be fully rested was a sensible strategy.

She glanced across to the chest of drawers. On top, nicely folded, was Sharon's Knight of the Round Table costume.

Yes, the charity walk. Four miles. It was a shame the costume didn't include a horse.

Just before nine, Jo was sitting down to a bowl of porridge and checking her food intake plan for the day. Along with plenty of fluids, it was porridge for starters.

Then, at ten-thirty, wholemeal toast with peanut butter and a very small portion of cold chicken pasta. And finally, three energy bars to scoff during the event.

She checked her phone's weather app. It would be warm – perfect for watching, not so perfect for doing. That said, hadn't she trained like an Olympic athlete for this?

*

Marilyn the tiger brought the red twelve-seater minibus to a halt by the busy meeting point behind the beach.

"Ooh, exciting," said Yvonne the pirate.

"Yes, it is," said Owen, looking relatively dull in his regular attire.

Jo, Knight of the Round Table, exited the vehicle with the others. In some ways, she felt bad about not having been a regular at the carnival, especially seeing so many families with curious children watching the many costumed and uniformed participants assembling. To have lived so near for so long and not taken an interest...

She smiled at Owen. They had been doing a lot of that during the journey, although things were hampered by having a pirate chatting away to them the whole time.

"Ruth says she's here," said Marilyn, checking her phone. Ruth had come by cab.

"I'll just get my stuff then," said Owen, heading off to a large box van belonging to Greg, one of the organizers who had brought some of the participants' larger items. In keeping with the incredible spirit of the event, Greg would also be doing the reverse run later.

Jo took it all in. While it was hardly Rio de Janeiro, it was shaping up to be a brilliant spectacle. In all, there were five flatbed trucks of various sizes, each decorated for a specific group. One carried a six-piece Dixieland jazz band, another the staff of a local supermarket dressed as Disney characters and ready with goody-bags for children. A third truck housed a string quartet, a fourth was home to a look-a-like waving Royal Family, while the last of them hosted a DJ blaring out what Jo understood to be 'bangers'.

She assumed that with a hundred walking contributors distributed between the trucks, onlookers wouldn't be subjected to a cacophony, but more a rise and fall of passing sounds.

As for those walkers, there was a marching band in uniform, some Royal Naval Lifeboat Institution volunteers pulling a rowing boat on wheels, a local keep fit club showing off their moves, people dressed as cheeseburgers for advertising purposes, scouts and guides, a posse of Star Wars Stormtroopers, Morris dancers, an assortment of circus clowns, and many, many more.

Meanwhile, Owen was getting his costume and shopping trolley from the back of the van. Not that it looked like a trolley. Dressed in cardboard and painted by Yvonne, it was now the Houses of Parliament on wheels, ready to be pushed by Big Ben.

"Hello everyone," said Ruth, emerging from behind a lorry. "Are we all here?"

"All here," said Marilyn.

"Including me," said Yvonne.

"A great effort, everyone," said Ruth. "Now, I've had a word with a marshal, and we'll be between the fourth and fifth vehicles."

"Is Alan coming?" Marilyn asked.

"He's over there, talking to Napoleon."

The man she indicated had his back to them but was unmistakeably dressed as a chef.

"I thought he actually was a chef," said Jo.

"Me too," said Yvonne. "I was about to order a hot dog."

Before long, Alan was joining them amid a flurry of hellos.

"Lovely to meet you," said Jo.

He doffed his hat to reveal a shiny cranium.

"You too, Jo. Ruth's been telling me all about you."

"Oh… good. She's something of a rock for the Go Club."

"Yes, she is. But what about you? How are you enjoying retirement?"

"I'm getting there. How about you? I hear you play bowls."

"Yes, indoor and outdoor. When I first retired I didn't know what to do with myself. Then, well… bowls isn't so much about the game; it's about getting out of the house."

"Makes sense."

"Righto," said Yvonne, "I'll be off now. See you all in a bit."

They waved her off with good wishes. She would be driving the minibus to the carnival's end point and then walking the short distance to the High Street to join them there.

"Is this your first carnival?" Alan asked Jo.

"Yes, it's great to be part of it."

And great to be part of the Go Club too.

She wondered – was this how true contentment worked? Instead of directly seeking happiness, was it more a matter of discovering meaning in life, and in doing so, finding a much richer kind of happiness?

*

It had taken a while to get going, but they were off! Okay, the front of the carnival was off. The Go Club's members, waiting between trucks four and five, took a while longer to start moving.

"Let's get collecting," called Ruth, shaking the Go Club's official bucket.

The starting point behind the beach, where many locals and tourists had gathered, saw plenty of coins clunking into various plastic buckets. Meanwhile, Owen was particularly successful in encouraging people to put their cash into the letterbox holes on either side of Parliament's roof.

The crowd then thinned as the procession very slowly followed the main road all the way along by the harbour and past the park. Eventually, they turned left over the old bridges which, in turn, brought them to the High Street – where the largest numbers of all would be lining the route on both sides of the road.

Suddenly, from out of the crowd, a pirate charged at them waving a cutlass.

"Yvonne!" the gang yelled.

Yvonne laughed. "My training schedule paid off. The carnival is halfway home and I feel as fit as a flea."

Jo, taking a turn with the collection bucket, gave a hearty "thank you" for each coin that clinked onto the others. It was going well, and it felt great to be part of something so worthwhile.

With plenty of noise, the parade trundled up the High Street and beyond, all the way to the station, and then round and back to the High Street, all the while waving and engaging with onlookers. For this final section, Ruth had the bucket.

"She's a good leader, isn't she," Jo told Alan.

"She is," he said. "That's probably why I keep out of the way. I hate to cramp her style."

"Is that the right thing to do though? To keep out of the way? Might you not look at her with pride, and want to be alongside her when she brings warmth and wise counsel into people's lives? Might it be good to think that's my Ruth, the best of us?"

"Possibly."

Jo smiled at him. "You're not in competition with her."

He nodded slowly, as if considering it.

Jo left him to it and moved alongside Marilyn.

"I'm tired, but it's been brilliant fun."

"I'm so glad," said Marilyn. "I've really wanted you to feel welcome, especially after your previous almost-retirement."

"Thanks."

Jo thought of poor Martin and everything that followed his passing. But it seemed more distant now – not so much in time, but in the wholly different life she was leading.

"We'll need a day off after this," said Marilyn.

"Yes," said Jo. Of course, that's how it would pan out for her. A day of rest at home on Monday before getting up early for Bonner's on Tuesday.

*

After an hour and forty-five minutes on their feet, the carnival was over.

"I don't think I could have gone much farther," said Ruth.

"Yep," puffed Yvonne, "another ten yards and you'd be scraping me off the pavement."

With a welcome breeze coming off the water, Jo beheld the quayside where hundreds were happily collapsing onto the grass glugging water and beer.

Alongside the pre-walk cash pledges, the money in the bucket looked good. And when Owen roughly estimated the money in the Houses of Parliament, everyone was confident they had exceeded all expectations.

"Well done, everyone," said Marilyn. "A brilliant effort!"

"Anyone free to take it to the bank tomorrow?" asked Ruth.

"I don't mind," said Owen.

Ruth smiled but then frowned.

"Didn't you have an essay to finish?"

"No, it's all done. It just needs a quick polish before going off."

"Very inspiring," said Yvonne.

"He almost inspired me," Marilyn told Jo. "I even downloaded a sample European History essay about the Coliseum. Then I thought why spend my money on studying when I could use it to see the actual place."

"Wow, what was it like?"

"No idea. Gavin wouldn't go."

Jo felt a sense of injustice.

"You should've gone anyway."

"Me? Visit Italy?"

"Yes. I'm up for a spot of travel. I mean we might not have the same interests. It's just a thought."

Just then, Alan returned from the minibus with a cooler box full of chilled beer, wine, and apple juice – and soon, overlooking the boats on the water, all had drinks.

Ruth raised her glass.

"To the Golden Oldies' Club and the future!"

All joined in.

"Only apple juice, Yvonne?" Owen asked.

"I'm making a positive start to the next twelve months," she said. "I finished this year six pounds lighter."

"That's great," said Ruth.

"Yes, well done," said Jo.

"It was nine pounds the year before," Yvonne reminded them, "so that's fifteen pounds in two years."

"We'll keep this going," said Marilyn.

"Thanks, because I intend to lose another ten by next June."

"Good for you," said Owen.

Jo concurred. Yvonne would falter occasionally, but she had friends who would support her all the way.

"Well, I think our little club is in very good shape," said Ruth. "We'll soon have Mandy and Mitch back, and now we have a lovely member in Jo. Could we all raise our glasses again. To Jo."

"To Jo," they echoed.

All except Yvonne, whose brow had furrowed.

"Have I missed something, Jo? I thought you were going back to work."

All the joy of the moment drained away.

"Yes… I'm thinking about it, but… they need me."

A brief silence descended on them.

"Well, best of luck," said Marilyn, breaking it.

"Yes," Ruth and Yvonne agreed.

For Jo, it was a relief.

"It's only for a year," she explained.

"Well," said Owen, "I'd better get my trolley over to Greg. Can't have it left here overnight."

She watched him head off to the box van that would take a number of the larger items away. But it didn't sit well with her. What if Owen went off without coming back?

In her mind, she ran up alongside him.

In reality, however…

Doubts arose.

But hadn't things changed? Hadn't she begun to rediscover something of her old self? And didn't that mean doing something?

Setting aside what others might think, she went after him.

"Need a hand loading it up?" she asked as she caught up.

There was only the briefest hesitation before he answered.

"If you like."

"I'm sorry I didn't tell you."

The Houses of Parliament came to a halt.

"No, it's okay. If anything, it's my fault."

"I don't understand."

"I spent half our time together telling you how you had to get retirement right before we could… well, you know the rest. The thing is, even as I was saying it I didn't want to put you off. My blinding logic usually gets in the way of things."

"No, you're wrong. You helped me to think, which is something I might not have done. Just imagine, I could be doing one of those 'A Hundred Things to Do Before You Die' lists."

"I don't mind if you go back to work. I'd still like to see you."

"Right… well… I'd like that too."

"Good."

Jo smiled. "I do understand the value of having the time to appreciate life. But going back to work at sixty-eight isn't a matter of rejecting a great gift. Bonner's value me and they need me. My old boss probably had me right when he named my greatest asset – loyalty. I've always been proud to be that person."

"Then Bonner's is a very lucky company."

She smiled and felt as free as one of the small sailboats bobbing merrily on the water. But somewhere in the back of her mind, it raised a question. Which way was the wind actually blowing her?

33

One Fine Sunny Morning

Stirring from her slumber, Jo gradually became aware of waiting for something. But what...?

Her alarm clock! She was waiting for it to buzz.

A moment later, for the first time in weeks, it did so.

She sat up. It was seven o'clock on Tuesday morning and she had a very busy day ahead.

It was a strange feeling. She had gone in to work on countless Tuesday mornings before, but this one felt utterly different. If anything, she was a little anxious.

She got out of bed and groaned at her legs still aching from Sunday's walk. Flexing her calves, she donned her dressing gown and pulled open the curtains on the new day.

"And so it begins... again."

Ten minutes later, she was downstairs enjoying a reviving cup of tea while the radio broadcast her regular classical music station. She would have a quick shower shortly and then some oat flakes, or possibly toast.

"No cooking or baking today, Mum," she told the photo on the worktop. "I'll be a bit busy."

As usual, time slipped away and she was soon out on the bright streets of South Tolcombe, walking the regular route, this time with a small, potted aspidistra in a carrier bag.

The sun was already pleasantly warm, suggesting a hot day ahead. How many times had she faced wind and rain… or sleet and snow? It was nice to have the weather on her side, especially as hurrying wasn't an option.

As ever, the journey was full of changing vistas – all so familiar to her. And as usual, crossing the footbridge, she slowed to admire the boats below.

She didn't stop though – there wasn't time. Instead, she pressed onward, across the main road and into the commercial sector.

Nothing had changed, although, after all these long years, the company would soon be gone from Avalon House.

In her mind's eye, she saw Bessie and a few others. They were by the entrance, laughing about something… and then they were gone.

She went in.

After signing in at reception, she headed up to the third floor. She would see Terry first. He was the reason she was there.

Outside the third-floor offices, she paused.

Take a breath…

The doors flew open and a young man, possibly in his late twenties, almost bumped into her.

"Sorry," he said on his way to the stairs.

She didn't know him. He didn't know her.

Entering the large main office, she beheld familiar faces – most of them smiling but perhaps also radiating a little bemusement. Of course, most of her regular day-to-day colleagues were on the floor above.

"Jo!"

Terry looked pleased at the door of his executive office on the far side and waved her over to join him. She said hello to a few people on the way.

"Come in, come in," he enthused.

As she did so, he closed the door for privacy.

"It's great to have you back. You're the safe pair of hands the company needs right now. Just bear with me a second..."

Watching him go to check something on his screen, she could feel it – that magnetic pull towards the firm. They needed her.

But this was a different Jo. One who could weigh forty years with Bonner's against something just as substantial. One who, on Sunday evening, settled the question of 'who is Jo Ramsey' while watching a cookery show on TV and looking up Italian getaways on her phone.

"Terry? Sorry to interrupt, but I haven't come back to work."

He looked up from the screen. There was a frown etched into his features.

"Sorry?"

"I've come to say thank you in person for giving me the chance to come back. But it's not for me."

She placed the new aspidistra on his desk.

"Jo...?"

"I've also come to say goodbye – not just to Bonner's, but to me. At least, the old me."

"I don't know what to say."

"You could wish me luck."

Terry nodded slowly. "I do wish you luck."

"You gave me an opportunity to come back to what I know. But I've found a whole other world out there and the sooner I embrace it the sooner I'll learn to make the most of it."

Terry puffed out his cheeks.

"You're sure I can't change your mind?"

"No, the clock's ticking. It never stops, does it. But what it's telling me is there's no time like the present to get started properly. Bye, Terry. And thank you."

He came round to give her a hug.

"Take care, Jo. And if you do change your mind..."

"I won't."

With gratitude, she smiled and left his office, closing the door behind her.

It felt liberating.

Outside the building's main entrance, the sun was shining on Tolcombe. And there, across the car park, was a red twelve-seater minibus.

Jo checked her watch.

9.15.

"Right on time."

Owen was standing beside the van's open side door, smiling as she approached.

"Room for one more?" she asked.

He nodded.

"We love you, Jo!" Yvonne yelled from somewhere inside. "But I hope you're suffering as much as the rest of us walkers."

"Don't worry, I am."

"We were worried you might change your mind," said Delia.

"Are you kidding?" Jo gasped. "I'm on my way to becoming a full member of the Go Club."

"That's the spirit," said Owen. "It's a whole new life."

"And don't look back?" she asked him.

"No, you should. Definitely."

Jo considered it and turned one final time.

Owen was right, of course. The firm as she knew it, with Bessie, Don, and all the others who were once so important to her, had long since faded into memory. At the end of forty long years, Avalon House was really little more than a concrete and glass structure. The true spirit of Bonner's lived on where it had always existed... in hers and Mr Bonner's hearts.

Turning back to Owen, her smile masked a tinge of sadness, but that was okay. She was still feeling elated at the text she had fired off to him yesterday, asking if he'd like to spend a week with her in rocky, rugged Cornwall for romantic walks, romantic dinners, and whatever other romantic notions came to mind. His response, it could be said, was extremely enthusiastic. Of course, she'd had to point out how this would have to wait as she'd first be spending a fortnight in Rome – the first week by herself on a cookery course, the second sightseeing with Marilyn, Ruth, and Yvonne.

"Ready to hit the road?" he asked.

She nodded and peered inside the minibus.

Marilyn was at the wheel.

"Well done, Jo."

Seated beside her, Ruth gave a little wave.

"Yes, *very* well done."

Jo's heart felt full of love.

"Sugar-free mint?" said Yvonne, proffering a pack.

"I'd love one, thanks."

And Alan was there too.

"I've decided to get more involved," he told her.

"I'm glad," said Jo, getting in.

It was still a bit daunting. For those worried about retirement, settling into it would always take a little extra effort. She'd gained something unexpected though – a group of big-hearted friends who chose freely to help and support each other. The Go Club. And Jo would be a loyal member for the rest of her days, however long that might be. If enjoying retirement was dependent on finding a purpose, then she had one.

As she settled into her seat, Owen got in alongside her and pulled the sliding door to with a clunk. A moment later, Marilyn steered them out through the gates.

"Watch out world, here we come!" Yvonne yelled through the open window.

Jo laughed.

Yes, watch out world…

With her laughter distilling into a hopeful smile, she turned to Owen.

"Well done," he said.

And as they squeezed hands, she knew this really was a new beginning… and that there was so much more to come.

The End

Thank you for reading The Golden Oldies' Club.

I don't have a giant publishing house working on my behalf so I'm reliant on good people like yourself to help me spread the word about my books. If you enjoyed reading this one and have a few minutes to spare, I would be eternally grateful if you could leave a review on Amazon. For feel-good fiction authors like me, it's the only way we can gain traction for our books (which allows us to write more books). It would make me very happy indeed if you were able to say something nice.

Thank you!
Mark.

For more info about me and my books,
please visit my website:

www.markdaydy.co.uk

Printed in Great Britain
by Amazon